GRIMLOCK TALES

J.J EGOSI

THE SILENT BANSHEE

I remember that evening well. Gunfire filled the cold air, and the ground squelched with my every fervent step.

Why must they always pursue me with one witch hunt after another? Do these fools not know the importance of understanding the occult?

I rushed through the forest, constantly looking over my shoulder as men with silver pistols fired at the slightest rustle or stir.

"Where is he?" one screamed. "He must be here somewhere."

The gunfire continued, tearing through everything that took refuge within the thickets—animals and humans, alike, had their fires of life snuffed out, their lifeless bodies forming a chorus of thuds.

A man with a myriad of gold ribbons and badges—the captain of the unit, or at least a high-ranking official—stood forward. His foot stepped across the corpse of a fox one of his men had put a bullet through. He sneered and pressed it into the mud.

"You're wasting your bullets. He isn't here."

"But how can you be certain?" a soldier asked.

"Simple," the captain replied with a devious grin. "Witches don't hide in plain sight and neither do their doctors; they sift through the shadows where we can't find them—or so they'd like you to believe."

The soldiers surrounded him with bewilderment plastered on their faces as he stared back while forcing the fox deeper into the ground.

"For just a moment in otherwise total darkness, you can find the pale silhouette. And when you do, you fire. Fire with everything you fucking have until you can no longer! Am I understood?" he yelled.

"Yes, sir!"

I heard it all from just several yards away. I peered over the tree's decrepit trunk, behind which I took haven.

They certainly are persistent... With a deep breath, I stepped out from the shadows. An ivory outline of my body made from smoke appeared as it always did, fading as quickly as it came as I returned to the mortal plane... *And quite ignorant of the occult.*

I smiled as I dusted myself off. *It takes little comprehension of my ways to ensnare me. Still, I have far too much work to do, and your foolish grasp is still too weak.*

I snapped my finger as if sending a bell through the forest that every soldier could hear.

"What was that?" One of them darted toward his left. "It sounded like a branch breaking."

"It could be him," another said. He ran to join the first, with his finger scraping the trigger.

The captain stepped forward, raising his hand to signal their halt.

"You shoot on my command."

A sharp breeze filled the forest as the soldier nodded.

Their breaths heightened, and gulps went around. Then, a whisper that chilled their blood swept past.

"That must be him," the captain whispered.

The forest fell to utter silence. The captain's eyes excavated every leaf, every stone, and every glimmer of light the insects left off. And then he saw it, just as he described but never had seen for himself: the ghostly outline of a man passing through the distant trees.

"There it is. Our king was right." The captain went pale, locked at the sight of me, with his feet unable to move his feet.

"Can we shoot now?" a soldier whimpered.

The captain gulped before nodding. "Nothing has changed. We came here with one purpose—one bounty assigned by the king, himself. And to collect, we must slay the witch doctor!"

I glanced back with a faint smile. I knew his chances of vanquishing me with paltry ammunition were as meager as his mind was ignorant.

The captain pulled the trigger. He shot at my ghostly appearance, piercing a dribbling hole in the center. The other soldiers followed suit, sending the air into a cacophony of ammunition that rattled the ground.

I inhaled their misfires with a smirk before peacefully slipping away into the forest to continue my work.

When you realize you're shooting blanks, perhaps then you'll realize there's more to human progress than simply extinguishing what doesn't make sense, I thought with a chuckle.

One thing I couldn't understand was their stubbornness. Could they not see what I was trying to achieve? Yes, calling me a witch was justified; I scoured the woods and streets in search of spirits. I was also a doctor, a seeker of paranormal solutions to problems so mundane by comparison. I wished no harm; quite the opposite. With my work, they'd see it soon enough. Furthermore, they could never stop me, for progress cannot be stopped.

The sounds of the soldiers faded into distant echoes as I advanced into the forest. I wandered on, unaware I was being pursued by another entity, something incorporeal, with a twinkling flame hovering toward me. I could feel its warm embrace. My heart sped without my realizing it.

"Who's there?" I spoke out loud.

I turned faster than the wind could blow, but was met with silence. The warm touch was gone. I looked around to ensure my mind wasn't playing tricks on me. After all, such occurrences were common in my line of work.

"It must have been my imagination."

"No, I'm just over here."

Her high-pitched voice over my head startled me. I nearly let out a scream, which she muffled with her hands across my mouth. She was a tiny spirit of sorts, hovering on black butterflying wings. She had pale skin and light green hair down to her shoulders. She was garbed in a white dress, shimmering like stardust under the moonlight piercing amidst tree branches.

I knew not what to say, even if she'd given me the chance. I'd never encountered such a creature before. She was enchanting, yet ominous, as she smiled back at me with intrigue.

"That was a neat little trick you pulled back there."

The tiny woman released her hands from my mouth, the smile on her face unchanging. I looked back, brimming with questions. There was but one I could ask.

"A trick?"

I looked at the vague remnants of the smokescreen I left behind. It was a mile away now, burrowing into the growing night.

"Are you referring to—"

"Not just that one, silly," she began, "I'm talking about all of it; you fade in and out of this plane, yet you're a human, right?"

I pondered her question with a puzzled look on my face. To say she could see through my ways was an understatement; even I lacked a proper answer.

"I'm human, yes. How I can do what I do still eludes me, however."

My mind took me back to a forest I found as a child, where a face with bright red eyes and purple flesh stared back with a grin. Before I knew it, I began to fade into a specter. Then, everything went dark...until it wasn't.

"I've possessed this ability for as long as I can remember. Perhaps a mutation of sorts from my line of work."

"Oh, and what sort of work do you do?"

"I study supernatural entities like yourself, actually." I looked at her with a hopeful smile. "Would you mind telling me what you are?"

She giggled back at me. "You're a funny man. You mean you study the supernatural, but you've never seen a wisp?"

"A what?"

Before I knew it, the air was filled with them, pale green and white lights hovering toward me like lanterns. They all stared back at me with gazes so alluring I couldn't break from them.

"I guess that makes sense," she told me. "We are rather small and difficult to find."

"And yet, there are so many of you." I estimated hundreds filling the air. I grew nervous that they would attract the soldiers' attention.

"Don't worry," another female wisp said. "No one will find us here."

"And where is '*here*' to you?" I wondered. "What does that mean?"

The wisps snickered, leaving me more stupefied. Were they referring to another world? Had I been transported to a different plane without my knowing?

"You're looking for supernatural creatures like us, aren't you?" the first wisp asked.

"Yes, that's right. I'm hoping to study...you. I mean...*them*. Perhaps even learn how to forge remedies to the various illnesses plaguing my kind.

"Like with magic and other stuff, right?" the first wisp asked.

"Essentially."

I smiled back as I began to warm up around them, not just from their flames, but from what I could gain with such a fortuitous encounter with a supernatural species that alluded even my research.

"Well, take the left-hand path down the nearest fork. You'll find this big old, abandoned mansion. Maybe some ghosts live there."

I scoffed with derision. "You must be the trickster sort. Even an amateur doctor would know that ghosts wouldn't dwell in such plain sight. Stories like that are told only to the children of my kind, I'm afraid."

"Is that so?" The wisp smiled. "You won't know if you don't look. There could be a major breakthrough in your work. Perhaps your work will be more respected among your peers, and you'll stop getting bombarded with bullets."

Her words were like a trance to me, as were the glowing gazes and their flames, pulling me in like a helpless moth.

"You could even learn about how you got that little power of yours."

Only now did I notice her heavy breath in my ear and that her fire glowed without ever burning.

"What do you think?"

I paused for a moment, contemplating her suggestion and

the possibilities it could offer me. This was an extraordinary opportunity, no matter the whimsy being shown, after all. I took a deep breath and nodded.

"I suppose it's worth investigating. Even if only the one time."

"Great!"

She flashed me a smile that I struggled to trust. Still, I felt her words were unbreakable. Guides in the endless night, I supposed these beings were. *Wisps. Living spirits of fire that lead the way.*

I followed the path just as she spoke. I could still feel their warm glow dimming with each step I took away from them. Could she have been telling the truth of what I thought to merely be a children's fairytale made flesh? What I knew for certain was there stood before me a fork as she described.

There were two dirt paths identical to one another; I didn't sense any supernatural force on either. I considered taking the right-hand path instead. What would await me if I did? I hadn't any idea, and that was just as exciting.

I saw something far down the left-hand path: a pale figure that wasn't of my own creation. It captured me in ways the other trail could never hope to achieve.

"Could it be?" I whispered. "Just as she said?"

I had no choice. Being a witch doctor, my integrity and curiosity about this world took me down the path with great urgency.

I marched over the fallen branches and past the fresh ones as my anxious eyes scoured the woods. In seconds, the figure down the path was gone.

Where did it go?

There came another voice—a weeping, this time. Then, she appeared: a pale woman fading in and out of the shadows.

Both her crimson gaze and her unbridled beauty froze me like the conifer lost to an unyieldling winter.

"Inconceivable," I began with a tremble, "for a creature of this magnitude to dwell in woods like these?"

She appeared just as gloomy as my research led me to believe; why...I couldn't figure out. Her inner wounds appeared to cut deep. We then locked dead stares, leaving my heart skipping a beat.

"You, there."

She can see me, too?

The woman forged a slight smile. She passed through the shadows faster than I could follow. In seconds, she passed through a hundred feet of thick woods and hovered beside me with that same milky complexion.

"Well, of course I can."

I was baffled in every way—by her speed and by her eyes. I began to question what I knew of her.

"Why are you crying?"

"Crying? Oh, right." The woman wiped her tears away. The droplets rolled off her face but did not fall to the ground; they hovered over her. I watched in awe as they disappeared into the night.

"Because I don't have a partner for this evening's tea party."

"A tea party?" I raised an eyebrow.

"Yes. All the others have partners, and I don't."

So, it's true? A weeping woman sifting in the light under an ivory veil. This woman's a banshee.

She looked back at me with a deep yearning. She leaned in so close I thought she'd pass through me next.

"Would you like to go to the tea party with me? Please."

"I don't much care for tea."

Why did I say that? Aside from tea being my favorite, this was just the sort of research I came here for—an encounter with a supernatural entity so elusive one only spoken of them in legends, yet there was mysterious doubt.

I shook my head, nodding off my previous response. "What I mean to say is I'd love to. Perhaps I could ask you a few questions, if you don't mind."

Her eyes lit up. "That would be fantastic! Come with me!"

She grabbed my hand and pulled me through the woods. The hairs on my skin rose as her chilling touch drove a shock through me, and I struggled to keep up with her.

"Where are you taking me?" was all I could ask as my breath shortened.

"To the tea party, silly. Come on!"

I was so overcome with confusion I struggled to maintain my thoughts. She passed through the trees as if they weren't there. The stones were nothing to her. And soon, I found they were nothing to me either. None of it was.

"Did I just"—

I passed through a tree, with no abilities of my own, as far as I knew. Could it have been the banshee's touch?

I could feel the physical world leaving me. Every leaf I reached for floated off into the night. The forest was as thin as air. Then, something appeared in the distance. Something the forest guardians had to tell me about before I could believe.

"A mansion? Out here?"

From the forest, we approached an expansive rolling field. The grounds were clad in banshees just like her, garbed in white dresses and heals, accompanied by their partners dancing under the moonlight. Many also gathered around the dozens of white-cloth tables where wisps would serve them tea.

Eclipsing it all was a familiar mansion. It seemed to have at least a hundred rooms. There was truly something damning about it. Its arched roofs were beaten down with the moon's glow as the windows with closed curtains shined back. The architecture was grim and dilapidated, peeling at the seams. Stone nuns guarded the entrance, something I swore I'd seen before. But where? I struggled to remember where I encountered such a grandiose estate in the middle of nowhere. In a newspaper, perhaps? An archive I found during my research? She then tugged on my hand again.

"Don't you go dreaming about me." I met her startling, wicked smile. "It's time for us to dance."

I couldn't shake off the feeling. Even those spirits around it felt familiar, yet I was convinced I'd never seen them. The floor brimmed with banshees and mortal men like me dancing under the night's glow with smiles and the wisps at their service.

"If you say so." That was all I could say. I was so perplexed, but the possibility of upsetting her terrified me.

I did as she wanted. We moved toward an open spot in the field and claimed it as our own. I led our waltz. Even with her heels, she was only as tall as my shoulder level. She leaned her head against me as I carried her through our dance. I felt taken away, somehow, as our steps moved with such grace. So light. So swift. I was pulled into a sense of bliss.

The physical world, wherever it had gone, was of no concern to me any longer. I loved every moment of holding her. I didn't even know her name, nor did I care to ask; I was so deep in love with the moment. The way she followed me, the way she felt, and the duality of the fall winds and wisp fires clashing against one another. That's all that mattered. All I wanted was an eternity of this precious moment.

"So, what do you think?" the banshee asked. "Have you been to a tea party like this one before?"

"As a matter of fact, I haven't," I replied, "nor did I think your kind really dwelled in such a place."

"You mean that nunnery?" she asked. "It's our home."

"A nunnery?"

The sense I'd come across the building was all the stronger and more irritating, itching at my mind. I didn't want to care. I wanted her.

"That's right," she replied. "You wanted to learn more about us, didn't you?"

My heart thundered at her words. "I only told you I wanted to ask you a few questions. How did you—"

"Because." She pressed her hands against my face and looked up with a suddenly vicious grin. "I can see right through you."

At that moment, everything became clear. I could remember where I'd first heard of this nunnery now—it was years ago during my research at an abandoned library in the city's lowest prefecture. Only the light of my lantern cut through the thick shroud of night.

I scoured the dusty shelves for reports of recent events when I came across a story of a nunnery that burned down with everyone in it during an attack by the witches years ago.

My trembling hands couldn't let go. That, I began to remember. I cross-referenced other texts, hearing rumors of the little girls that perished haunting that mansion as its incorporeal protectors. It appeared they'd aged—even in the afterlife—into irrefutable beauties capturing my heart and gripping me in fear.

I tried so hard to forget. I was certain this couldn't have been true. I'd surely be the first to know of such an occurrence. I then focused back on my present events, staring at the nunnery before me. It was just like the one in the photos before the fire, yet there were no effects of the ruthless inferno.

I began to shake. The pieces I thought were adding up were spreading further away. Where was I, really? Was I actually taken into another world?

I slowly and hesitantly turned toward the other banshees, then saw the banshees unhinge their jaws and hold their partners by the faces. The faces of the banshees altered into horrifying hideousness—nothing close to resembling a human, more like wicked hags. They each let out a vicious scream that turned my blood to ice. I felt her frozen touch now as I turned to face her again.

There was no way to escape her wicked grin. A part of me still didn't want to, yet I knew there was something horrific at work.

"That was quite the evening, you know—being burned alive all those years ago."

"I wasn't responsible for that. I swear—"

"Here's something a witch doctor may be interested to know."

I looked toward the other banshees, trying to break from her stare. What I saw was worse: men being drained of their lives, turning utterly gray and emaciated. They were depleted without mercy.

She pulled my face back, digging her talons into my cheeks as I fought to break free.

"A banshee's scream can age a man to the brink of death as a reminder of the years taken away from us."

It was over for me. I could feel her resentment toward that fire burning down on me like an unforgiving sun.

The banshee smiled again. "Some say banshees are actually silent. You tell me...if you can."

I couldn't. With a single howl, I'd gone deaf. The years sped beyond my desperate grasp as I began to age into oblivion until I was gone, silent like the vengeful banshee that took me away.

VAMPIRES IN ELANDOR

With the night still young, the streets of Elandor bustled with merriment all around, people traveling side by side and in groups with their coats buttoned and their smiles illuminating the air.

"A beautiful night, isn't it?" he asked.

I sat in the back of a horse-drawn carriage, watching the cobblestone pass me by. I was adorned in my best suit and held a sheet of parchment upon which a poem left by my admirer was scribed.

"Yes, I suppose it is."

I slid my finger over where she left her ruby lips printed by her signature.

"I take it you have a big night ahead of you, sir."

"I was proposed to, if you could believe it," I told the rider. "I'm actually on my way to see her at the royal ball she's hosting."

"Royal, huh?" The man smiled. "You're a lucky man."

"I'd certainly say so," I replied. "Strange thing is, I've never met her. I only received this letter."

"Really?" He veered over his shoulder for a moment to

make certain by my gaze that I wasn't joking. "And if you don't mind my asking, what do you do? Being proposed to by a royal you've never met isn't the sort of thing that happens to common folk, you know."

"Well, I think you'd laugh if I told you," I replied with a nervous look.

"Maybe I would. All questions are worth asking, aren't they?"

I pondered his reply with a smile. "That, they are. And to answer your question, I guess you could say I work with medicine."

The man smiled. "That explains it. There's always money to be made in that field...and female suitors, of course."

"I don't do it for the money or the women," I replied, "but for the love of finding cures. And it's mostly research so far."

"Either way, it sounds you've taken this woman's breath away."

I looked down at the image she sent me—long, flowing hair as red as her lips. Her eyes were sultry as they were fierce, illuminating her pale skin.

"It was an even exchange, then."

The man nodded, impressed. "Do have a picture I could see?"

"Of...?" I responded.

My gaze was momentarily taken toward something looming in a nearby alleyway, something dark and lumbering like a shadow piercing toward me. What was it?

"The charming lady."

His words broke my train of thought, and as soon as he did, the entity vanished. I was bewildered, but oddly relieved.

"Sure. Just be sure to focus on the road," I replied with a nervous laugh as I leaned forward and handed him the picture attached to the note. The man took it and stared for a moment, puzzled.

"So, what do you think?"

"Hmm. I'm not sure what you want me to say. All I see is a mirror and a vanity desk."

My eyes widened. "I beg your pardon?"

"Here"—he handed the picture back to me—"there's no woman that I can see."

"You mean you can't see the beautiful woman with cascading red locks and glistening lips?"

"No, but I'd love to," he replied with a chuckle.

I looked down at the photo and could see her plain as night. Why couldn't he? I studied the note with instructions I needed to follow prior to my arrival—to collect an old heirloom.

"Find the vermilion jewel that was taken from my blood-line, and my hand will be yours, eternally," I recited under my breath.

"Did you say something, sir?" the man asked.

I looked toward my right where I saw an antique jewelry store.

"Here's fine."

"Excuse me?"

"I can walk the rest of the way."

Despite the protesting look on his face, he complied and pulled the carriage to a halt. I paid the man thirty silver coins from my burlap sack before stepping off the carriage. I was certain he was bewildered, as were many of the townspeople watching me step off a carriage in the middle of a busy street.

"Hey, watch where you're going!" a woman shouted.

"You'll cause an accident!" a man added.

I rushed past the oncoming people and horse-drawn carriages, narrowly escaping collisions.

I didn't have interest or time for the ruckus, not until I

reached the store and the people gathered around. Not until I had answers.

"Excuse me, ma'am."

The woman rolled her eyes at me. "Look, whatever the reason for trying to cause a collision, I don't have time."

"I'm looking for a vermilion jewel."

"Vermilion?" Her eyes widened.

"Yes, like her hair."

I showed her the image of my bride. The woman responded with the same befuddled glare the driver wore when he saw it.

"There's no woman in that picture. Something tells me you've gotten hit sprinting through traffic before."

She can't see her, either? I looked down at the photo and crinkled it in my hands. I didn't say another word; I simply pushed her aside and moved beyond.

"Hey, what the hell was that for?!"

"Sorry!"

I walked into the jewelry store with two missions to complete, the first being to find this heirloom stolen from her family. Where it could be, I didn't know, nor did I know why she'd suspect I could find it. Was I placing a slipper or pulling a sword like in those old tales? It certainly felt like that.

The second mission was to find anyone who could see the woman in the photo. I was met with heads shaking left to right each time I asked. Faces were growing more unfriendly. Soon, I was being met with scowls.

Despite growing dizzy from rejection, I never looked away from the jewelry on display. Many items were large and glowing. However, none would glow red for me. I approached the last person I hadn't yet—a scowling clerk.

"Excuse me. Do you mind if I ask you a few questions?"

She sighed at me. "If no one else can see her, I don't think she exists."

"I also wanted to ask about a vermilion jewel. Would you happen to possess something like that here?"

"A vermilion jewel?" She looked at me with intrigue as she turned around. "Let me see if I have something like that in the back."

"It's for my bride-to-be, so please hurry."

"You mean the woman in the photo?" The clerk groaned and stopped in place before turning toward me. "I told you she isn't real."

I could feel my face turning as red as the shade I sought. I looked around the jewelry store and could only see liars.

What's happening here? I thought. *This is more than me running into traffic. Are they conspiring against me because they know of my work?* I was certain what I did was kept secret from civilians.

I gritted my teeth and stormed out of the shop and down the streets in search of an explanation.

I've had many paranormal encounters in the line of what I do, but never a woman that doesn't appear in photos.

I wanted nothing to do with the townspeople, who couldn't see what I could. They'd served their purpose for now. I, instead, followed the dirt path down the outskirts and headed for the woods.

And yet, I'm able to see her. How is this possible?

I moved down the winding trail where few traveled. My mind was wrapped around the conundrum when I heard a voice: *"Find me in the shadows, darling...where the jewel of my heart's calling."*

I froze in place. The words echoing around pierced through me like daggers. I couldn't even realize the worried gazes on me; I only thought of her voice. I stared down at the picture, certain the woman in it was speaking to me.

"Come where the bats flutter, where the trees sway and the bushes mutter."

"Where the bushes mutter?" I asked.

Her voice entranced me. I followed it down the path, listening intently as it grew louder. Soon, I found myself alone, walking around the forest's borders where the shrubs beneath me seemed to call my name.

"I know she's here. She isn't make believe."

"Satisfy the cusp of your bereavement. Grasp your reality and find me this evening."

I gulped to calm my anxiety. My fingers itched as they tried to reach for something—what exactly, I wasn't sure. I didn't understand what she spoke of, yet each word was more hypnotic than the last.

"What's this?"

I saw something glow just inches from my feet. It grew brighter when I acknowledged it. My eyes lit up. It was the vermilion jewel!

I leaned down and reached into the bush, following the illuminating shade until my fingers slid against its warm and smooth surface. I plucked it out from the branches, and there it was, at last.

So, it does exist, I thought, *which means so does she. But where?*

I looked down at my flawless reflection. It was like staring at my face in frozen blood. It was so deep. So pure. Suddenly, another face appeared behind me. I went pale at the sight of her.

"Looking for me, are you?"

I immediately turned around. A gust of bats fluttered through the air, blanketing the moon hanging over her head. Her smile was so contagious. She wore spiked stiletto heels and a long black dress with a slit down her right leg. Her collar was like her sleeves—clad in spider-like claws arching out.

She was just like in the photo; there was no denying it. No conceivable way anyone could tell me this woman didn't exist.

"You're the one that wrote me that note."

"So, you tracked me down?" She smiled. Her fangs glowed under the moonlight. "I'm pleased to know mortals like yourself can still see my alluring gaze even after eight hundred years."

Eight hundred years?

I was flabbergasted. She spoke with such conviction. Everything about her was so mystifying. There was no chance I could look away.

"Just what are you?" I asked. "And why have you chosen me?"

"You needn't worry about my reasons. I simply fancy human males like yourself, is all."

"The way you speak, too"—a smile formed across my face —"I'm certain you aren't human. You're a—"

"A vampire," she finished.

The bats over her head shrieked with delight as she unfurled her black, spiked wings—just like theirs.

"And I take it you're enthralled."

Indeed, I was. I'd studied vampires all my life. They were one of my favorite subjects in stories in childhood—crimson prowlers of the night that fed on mortals to sustain their youth for centuries. I always wanted to meet one.

"Well, don't just stand there," the vampire said, "we have a ball to go to."

I was taken from my train of thought. I gulped before looking down at the jewel still in my hold.

"May I ask one thing? What exactly is this stone to you?"

She met me with a sneer. I could tell my question bothered her to a degree. Still, I wanted to press on for my curiosity.

"You told me this was an heirloom of your people. Was it taken from you? Perhaps by other humans?"

The vampire smirked. "You're intuitive, and you ask a lot of questions. Exactly my favorite kind of man."

"Well, it comes with what I do for a living." I nodded and laughed, blushing.

"I can tell you reserve your time for the stranger aspects of the living. Isn't that right?"

"If you mean the occult, then yes. I'm—"

"I've drained many humans before. Thousands. But you...I think I'd like to hold on to you for as long as I can. Maybe even feed you some of what makes me so"—She suddenly vanished into the night before appearing behind me. Her talons rolled across my shoulders as she leaned in to whisper, "Captivating."

I gulped before looking into her gaze. What did she mean? Did she desire to make me a servant of hers? Indentured toward the act of the hunt for blood and eternal youth? I could only lose myself in the allure of fangs dancing toward my neck, tapping lightly as I shivered at her touch.

"I'm joking, of course." She pulled her teeth back, giving me an odd sense of relief. "We've only just met, after all."

"Right."

"But I'm certain you're the one for me. The man who found the jewel taken from us long ago."

"So, it's very important to you?"

"Of course. Now, come with me." She took my hands and pulled me into the air with her. My heart raced as I left the ground, climbing higher toward the moon. "The ceremony of our love awaits us."

It felt like a dream. I hovered through the night sky, feeling the misty breeze against my face as she carried me away. Yet, it also felt like a twisted nightmare. Bats swarmed around us by the tens of thousands. The air began to stain with the smell of blood. As we soared over the city, people below us fled in terror at the sight of the vampire.

She snickered to herself. "Scaring humans never grows old, does it?"

She looked over at me with a smile. I wasn't sure what to say. Did she want me to agree? Admittedly, I agreed with her. A part of me enjoyed frightening the simple away with my profession, and to fly beside a vampire was a declaration of that. Together, we soared toward wherever my crimson bride-to-be would take us.

"Look over there. We're not far now."

She pointed to a towering castle in the center of an open field. It was pitch black, with a spiked iron fence around. In the front was a lavish garden centered with a fountain adorned with stone bats and gargoyles. Pouring down from the mouth of a weeping mortal woman was blood. Hundreds of wooden horse-drawn carriages approached the castle's gates and parked on the premises, with vampires stepping off. Their glow under the moon was far from human, and the gleaming fangs were even more clear.

"You certainly have a wide circle of connections."

"I'm a princess, so of course word of my marriage gets around."

"And your kind doesn't always choose to fly?"

"Most of us like to be subtle," she replied. "You can't really tell we're vampires unless we make that part of us known."

"I see."

I imagine she did so with me in more ways than one, so that there was no confusion. No doubt of the sort of woman she was.

We descended toward the stone footsteps surrounded by an array of various flowers. I looked around and laid my eyes on a field of black roses. Flecks of white hung from the petals like the moon had dusted off of them.

"Here you are." I plucked one from the ground and

offered it to her. "It isn't much of a gift, but I've never been good with gifts."

She smiled back at me. "You're my gift...as is the jewel you retrieved for me."

She took the rose from my hand and inhaled the intoxicating aroma. She snapped the head off and placed it on her dress and tossed the stem into the fountain before walking toward the entrance.

"But I do love a black rose."

She knocked on the door. My heart pounded as I heard footsteps approach from inside. *Just what are other vampires like? Are there all as ancient and alluring?*

The door opened and attracted the attention of the vampires inside. They all appeared related to her, bearing red hair and pale complexions. The males were clad in pristine suits and the women in dashing dresses.

Perhaps this is how they all appear.

There was still so much I wanted to know. At last, I'd have the chance.

"I see you made it here without the humans chasing you down," a young male said. "Seems you've learned your lesson."

"As if," she replied with a smirk.

"And you brought your husband with you," a female vampire said with a glowing smile.

"Yes, and look what he brought."

She took my hand and raised it for them to see the vermilion.

They all flashed nefarious grins at me, putting their fangs on display as they leaned closer. My bride must have been doing the same, but I was too nervous because of their lustful eyes to realize it, too fearful of what I may have walked into.

"These are my dear relatives. They traveled hundreds of miles for this special day."

"A pleasure." I bowed my head. The many vampires chuckled in response.

"They'll take us to the ceremonial chamber," she replied.

I nodded along with a blank gaze as she took my hand. Together, we followed her relatives through the foyer with tapestries depicting what appeared to be their royal ancestors. We entered a hall clad with more art. Each way I turned were faces of those that appeared to have lived before her. All I could think of was my current state.

What exactly had I agreed to? I thought. *She's beautiful, yes. Like no mortal woman.*

I looked at her crimson eyes and was stuck in her gaze.

Yet, we've only just met. I don't even know her name, I thought as I began to recall the image she sent me. *I was the only one that could see her. And I did find her jewel. Perhaps this is fate.*

I was as hopeful as I could be amidst my impulsive decisions to pursue such a temptress. I was then met with distant music, strings playing a dreary and haunting tune that loudened with each step we took toward the source. Eventually, the double doors ahead of us flew open and there it all was on display for us.

Hundreds of vampires slowly swayed their hips to the music. They drank from goblets of blood with smiles on their faces as anthropomorphic cats and bats played their cellos and violins for as long as their masters wished.

It was all so incredible—better than any tale I could have read. To see so many vampires up close and be a part of their evening...I never wanted to leave.

My eyes met with the chamber's back wall where a black throne spiked with claws and fangs sat in the center. I then remembered something else my soon-to-be-bride told me, something that had slipped my mind.

"You said you were a princess. Is that correct?"

"And when my yearning intervenes, my heart shall make me queen."

She tossed me into the throne with such force, she nearly knocked the wind out of me. I looked at her with a baffled stare. All the vampires looked back with unnerving grins. The music suddenly died; only the sound of my heart and their heels stepping toward me filled the room.

"What's going on here? I thought we were getting married."

"You still don't get it."

She lunged herself on top of me. I could feel her knee digging between my legs as she placed her tightening hands on my shoulders. Every part of my being trembled as her eyes locked with mine.

"You foolish mortal man. Our weddings are nothing like yours."

She slid her tongue around her neck with a grin. I could feel myself being trapped with no way out of her gaze.

"And this here"—she snatched the jewel out from my hand—"is no ordinary jewel."

"What are you saying?"

"I'm going to use it to make a baby with you."

My eyes widened. I was positive I'd misheard, yet her conviction told me otherwise. "A baby?"

"Yes. What do you say, my darling?"

She slid her nails across my cheek as the other vampires watched, salivating at the sight of her touching my human skin.

"I don't think I'm ready. Apologies." That was all I could think to say. Had she gone mad?

"Let me help with that, then."

She leaned forward, digging her knee deeper. I could feel intense pain soaked in pleasure as her fangs reached toward my neck.

"How's that?"

"This is only our first meeting, you said that yourself. Don't you think this is short notice?"

"Are you telling me *no*?"

She pulled back her fangs and knee with a sneer. Yet, my doubts were drained. I lusted after the pain and pleasure she'd given me.

"I would never."

"Wonderful."

As she dug herself back into her position, the other vampires clapped with excitement. The cats and bats played their strings again.

"There's just one thing you might want to keep in mind."

"Whatever it is, I'll accept it. For you," I replied.

My consciousness began to slip as she pulled me deeper with her every word. I was truly enthralled and unable to think about anything but her.

She smiled at me.

"This is a special marriage. For once a child is born, the human that spawned it will be no more. So comes your tragic end, my fallen love. So quick. So arousing. All under the sharp embrace of the vampires in Elandor."

She was right. Every bit of what she spoke was true. The vermilion flashed, and her teeth sunk into my flesh. Fleeting as the sensation was before it came to a halt, I adored every waking moment of it.

KEY TO THE FIEND'S GATE

As usual, the thick mist blanketed my walk by the shipyard. Boats bustled with merchants hauling their shipments. I'd hear the same exchanges I heard every night, manic shouts from the boss to his slow employees.

I'd become somewhat desensitized—rather, I didn't care, especially not on this occasion. This evening, I was expecting a most peculiar liaison.

How many years has it been?

I rummaged through my trench coat pocket and recovered a rolled-up sheet of parchment. Upon it was a letter with the signatures of my three friends from my days at the Miskeritonic Academy.

Five years now? Perhaps longer?

I glanced at the photos tacked toward the bottom. I supposed they attached them, figuring I'd forgotten what they looked like. They were wrong. I could also remember our lessons from long ago as I traversed through the cobblestone streets.

I remembered being in the middle of an evening lecture.

We were the only students to be taught at such an hour. I chose these sessions to avoid the distraction of other students. However, the other three, admittedly a bumbling trio, waited until there were no other available slots, and that's how our fates crossed.

***

"Hey. Hey, can you hear me?"

"I hadn't gone deaf, have I?" I peered over my shoulder at my friend, a forced acquaintance at the time. He'd tap my shoulder with the feather of his quill. Sometimes, he'd even jab it in my ear to get my attention.

"What did you get for this question?" he asked.

I looked at the scribbling on his assignment with a dim stare. Dumbfounded, he'd offer such an equally dim response.

"First off, that's for the wrong class."

"Are you sure?"

"Second, the question is asking you to compare a healing remedy native to the elves to one used by fairies. Why are you just talking about your fascination with trolls?"

"Because they're badass, my friend. Mystics of the woods with rank breath that eat whoever crosses their boundaries."

"Interesting you identified with that creature," I muttered as I rolled my eyes. *Does he really aspire to be a troll?*

"Orcs are way better," the friend beside me whispered. "They're much larger and wield huge clubs."

"That doesn't mean you have to take up the space of an orc." His arms and legs couldn't have been more spread out, nor could his books have been more scattered. He was an utter slob. I scooted my seat a foot to my right to keep my distance, not knowing I'd be moving closer to my note-tossing friend on the other side.

"Everyone knows goblins are the coolest."

My friend tossed a few crumpled notes at my forehead. I

unrolled each one, already sure they'd depict goblins slinging rocks at villagers.

I sighed and clenched my quill to keep from smacking any of them. "None of this has anything to do with our lesson on demon species!"

My raised voice grabbed the attention of the professor on the other side of the classroom. She stared back with a raised eyebrow.

"It appears I'm interrupting you delinquents, I see."

"No, ma'am." I rose from my seat with the most apologetic expression I could muster. Sweat rolled down my face.

"So you say?"

I shook as my friends snickered. I could not shake the professor's stare. She aimed her wooden pointer at the diagram. "There is a litany of different demons races said to exist across the world. The exact number varies as they continue to crossbreed..."

I gulped and nodded, feeling her question approaching. I hoped, for my sake, I'd have the answer for her.

"...can you tell me what the four core races of demonkind are?"

I took a sigh of relief.

"Yes, in order from smallest to largest: *imp*, *gremlin*, *fiend*, and *devil*. Imps play the role of messenger in the hierarchy. Gremlins are the servants, fiends are the masterminds, and devils are rogue cannibals that stand as the apex predators of demonkind."

My professor smiled and nodded. "Very good. At least someone's getting something out of my classes."

I took my seat, basking in the feeling of accomplishment. I continued to take my notes as she proceeded with the lecture. My friends leaned forward with a round of snickers.

"That was a close one, wasn't it?" said the friend on my left.

"No thanks to you knuckle draggers," I replied.

"We're just having fun, you know. How else can we pass time through this boring lecture?" my friend on my right continued.

"Well, if you paid attention, you may learn something interesting," I told him sternly.

My friend behind me groaned. "How can anyone focus when our professor's so endowed in the chest?"

"Not to mention her hips and thighs are to die for," my friend on the left spoke.

"And her ass is incredible," was the response from my right-hand side. "If only she'd turn around more often."

"You three will end up retaking the harassment course if you keep talking like that," I told them.

"You think she'll be the one to teach it?" my friend behind me asked.

"No," I said with a groan as I tried to keep up with my notes, writing more zealously as she moved her way toward our desks.

"Here she comes." They giggled.

"I have your exam scores from last week."

"How'd we do?" my friend on my right asked with a wink.

"Pathetic as always."

She tossed their exam results on their desks without a second glance. Their scores seemed to only be getting lower.

"Hey, we got a hundred points," my friend on my left said.

"Between the three of you." I rolled my eyes.

"And another perfect score for the one person who seems to actually give a shit in this class."

She smiled as she handed me my exam result. I blushed and nodded before taking it from her hands.

"Well, you know. I try," I said with a nervous laugh.

As she walked back to the board, I could feel the jealousy of my friends piercing through me.

"How do you always get such great scores?" my friend to my left asked.

"I study and take a genuine fascination with my work," I replied. "You should try that if you're looking to improve."

"You mean you're interested in demons?" my friend to my right asked with a disgruntled glare.

"Not just demons." I smiled. "All things supernatural. It's all so intriguing. Their behavior, ecology, appearance, all of it. Especially the stories I'd remember hearing when I was a kid. I don't know how anyone couldn't adore them. There's still so much humanity doesn't know yet. So many ways we could benefit from such knowledge."

"Wow, you're quite the fanatic. You talk about the supernatural like we talk about women," my friend behind me said before they burst into suppressed laughter to avoid the professor's attention.

"I suppose you're not wrong," I replied.

I could feel myself coming to life around them as I spoke of my passion, tolerating them for that moment.

"How about you help us study for the next exam? We can talk about this stuff...and women. What do you say?" my friend to my left asked.

I pondered the question for a moment. I was rather hesitant to spend any more time with them than I needed to.

"I go to the library from ten to three each evening. You can find me there."

"Make it the tavern down the street and you have yourself a deal," my friend to my right said with an elbow nudge.

I rolled my eyes and accepted the deal despite being unprepared for it.

What awaited me was a night of antics. Of being in a loud and crowded room with an overpowering stench of liquor. We all drank our fill of liquor. My friends flirted with each woman that passed, missing their target each time. All the while, I could still teach them something.

I remember them initially failing their exam and having to take additional courses to pass. They didn't perform as badly, however, and we all eventually graduated. I had seen none of them since, nor had they written to me. Losing touch was disappointing since I had grown quite fond of them. Against all odds, I enjoyed the time we shared in the tavern that night.

***

On this night, I waited for them at the counter of that same tavern many years later.

They said they wanted to meet me here at midnight. Where are they?

I read the note they gave me as I took a sip from my tankard. A sense of doubt kicked into me. I grew worried they'd gone and tricked me.

A tall bartender with pale blue-and-white chin-length hair approached me. He wiped down a tankard with a cloth.

"Stood up, I see."

I looked at the clock in the room. It was one-thirty now. I took a deep sigh.

"I suppose you could say that."

"A shame to hear that. Can I get you another drink?"

"Make it a whiskey." I slid my tankard toward him. "Neat, please."

"As you wish."

As he refilled my tankard, I heard an interesting discussion at the table nearest to me. I leaned in to eavesdrop on the six fishermen's conversation.

"That's the eighth case just this week. Where do you suppose they're going?" one of them asked.

"I don't know. There's been at least three hundred people

that have disappeared since last month and no sightings of their bodies anywhere," another said.

"They must be buried rather deep at sea if even we can't find them," another said, trembling.

They all nodded and downed their rounds of beer, as if hoping to intoxicate themselves beyond the point of fearing being the next to sink.

"Your drink, sir."

I was so lulled by their conversation I didn't feel the bartender tapping my shoulder.

"You wanted a whiskey, right? Neat?"

My eyes widened when I connected with his presence. I spun around with an ardent nod.

"Yes. Apologies." I took the tankard from the counter and took the first quarter in a single gulp before putting the tankard down.

"You're quite the drinker," he said with a smile.

"I'm just a little worn, I suppose. Preparing myself for an encounter that never was, after such a long day of work."

"And what do you do?"

I took another sip. "I work in medicine."

"Really? I took you for the detective sort."

"You could say I get involved with rather unusual cases from time to time. I work with the supernatural. My goal is to find cures for the rampant illnesses in our world by better understanding the other species we share it with."

"So, you're a witch doctor?" The bartender smiled. "We don't get many of those around here."

"Well, it's not a very respected field, now it is?" I took my next sip with derision before placing my tankard again down.

"I meant no harm by that," he said. "How about I make it up to you by showing you some artifacts?"

"Artifacts?" I raised my eyebrow at the rather bizarre

suggestion. Paired with the idea of a bartender owning anything magical, I was certain I was being fooled again.

"Yes. Just a few things my father used to collect when he was a witch doctor."

"You mean to say he worked in my field?" My eyes immediately widened.

"He sure did." The bartender smiled. "He passed away not long ago but left me all his collections. I keep them down in the tavern's cellar."

"That's a rather odd place to keep such possessions," I replied.

"It's safer than my house if you could believe it. My wife always threatens to throw them out. Trinkets, as she calls them."

"I see." I smiled as I drank the last of my whiskey. "I think I'll take you up on your offer."

He nodded with a grin. "Wonderful. Let me just find someone to cover for me."

The bartender tapped the shoulder of a woman with green and white hair and whispered in her ear. I was certain they winked when they smiled at each other. I didn't know what it meant; I was more curious to see how I could salvage the night my supposed friends besmirched.

I was led toward a door, which he opened with a twist of the knob. On the other side of the door, I was met with a dark downward staircase caked in cobwebs and scurrying rats.

"Ignore the mess. Most of them will be used for experimenting, anyway."

"Oh, it's no problem." I followed him down the creaking steps. "My study chamber's a mess, as well."

My mind suddenly rang with something I'd missed. He spoke of experimenting. For what purpose, exactly? Did he mean that? My mind became engulfed with many questions, each more troubling than the last. Before I could find the answers, the door shut behind us, leaving us at the mercy of the dim, candlelit staircase.

"This way," he told me.

I held my breath and followed. We moved down, each step like a pounding against my heart. I heard more than scurrying; I heard screams and snickering.

The candlelight brightened when we entered a long hall with many doors on either side. The floors and walls were stained with blood and some with scratch marks of what I could only fathom were people trying to escape.

I shook with incredible horror as I walked beside him. I was certain proceeding was a grave mistake, but my curiosity led me.

"I think you'll be really impressed with the sorts of trinkets he held onto. Too bad he's no longer around. I bet you would have gotten along."

His tone grew more sinister without my knowing. Had I recognized the shift before, would I have followed him?

The door to our left opened and short men and women rushed out. Upon close inspection, I realized the four-foot creatures were green and white and had horns and tails. I immediately recognized them from my lecture long ago.

"Those creatures. They're gremlins, aren't they?"

"Yes," the bartender said, as he looked over at me. "They're quite helpful in preserving my father's things."

"They're servants, is what you're saying?" I asked with a gulp.

"I wouldn't go that far. I'd probably get in trouble with the government if they thought I had that sort of arrangement," he said with a laugh.

From out of the rooms on either side, tinier creature fluttered their wings. They were humanoid but with horns and tails. Their hair was a deep shade of red, with black streaks running through.

"And those are imps," I began. I recalled them on the diagram clear as day, watching them hover over me.

"Huh?" The bartender's eyes widened before registering what I'd said. "Yes, they sort of come with the territory of having gremlins working for...I mean, *with* you," he said with another laugh. "They make great—"

"Messengers," I said with sunken despair across my face.

He stopped and looked back at me, puzzled by my expression, before smiling.

"Well, I suppose they do collect my parcels from time to time."

His tone seemed to have relaxed, almost brushing off any fear he sensed in me. Perhaps he enjoyed it. He moved down the hall, and I was given no choice but to either follow or be at the mercy of his demonic acolytes.

I was taken aback by his nonchalance and my thundering heart while the hall filled with demons rushing in and out of every chamber.

I couldn't see everything inside; I saw just enough— bodies strapped against surgical tables and tortured where they laid. Scalpels and drills and many other tools, all drenched in blood, were scattered beside them as shadows of horned beasts arched over with haunting smiles.

Another dread-inducing thought filled my mind. This could have been what the sailors spoke of! This had to be where the missing people were taken. If my deduction was right, it meant one thing for me.

"Who are you?"

The bartender grinned and peered over my shoulder. His once blue eyes faded into a vicious shade of black.

"Just a man with a cellar...and a key."

He pulled a golden key from his sleeve and flashed it at me. He pointed it toward the center door in front of us, and his talons stretched, releasing a black mist from the tips.

"You care to see what's inside, don't you?"

I stumbled back. My mortified heart refused to give in, even as screams emanated from the halls, hammering into my mind. They grew louder—like a tempest trying to drown me in their suffering.

He stared back at me with a growing smile as I trembled. My eyes widened, and I began to hyperventilate. I couldn't allow myself to be another.

I turned and darted toward the exit.

"You can't take me!"

Before I could make it over five feet, a tugging around my ankle sent me to the floor. I screamed as I fell face first.

I looked down with a sense of hopeless defeat. Tears began to roll down my eyes as I looked at my reflection in the blood trickling from my jaws. The tugging strengthened, pulling me toward the door. It didn't feel like a hand. What was it? I was too afraid to look, but I had to know. I glanced over my shoulder and saw a barbed blue tail pulling me. With his tail and curved horns, the bartender's true form was revealed.

I knew what he was—a fiend. I couldn't bring myself to say it, nor would it have helped me in the slightest.

With a devious smile, he placed his key through the hole of the wooden door and turned it to the right. I could hear the lock opening and my future closing. He snickered as he pushed the door open. What awaited on the other side, however, was far worse than anything I could have fathomed in my mind.

The chamber was drenched in blood and bones; the fetid stench permeated the air. In the center was an iron stake with three bodies nailed across it. I instantly recognized the bodies of my three friends from the academy, lifeless, torn, and stitched together, staring at the ceiling with hollow eye sockets.

I was so furious yet petrified as the fiend's tail tightened around my ankle, cutting off the circulation and certain to cut off more soon enough.

"Father's work was quite impressive. But not as impressive as mine."

I gulped and dug my nails into the floorboards as I tried to crawl away. I stared at the many trails left before me, and a sense of futility set in. He laughed as he watched me struggle until I could no longer.

"You know, it's rude to say your friends stood you up when they didn't. They're right here. And now, you can be with them forever."

I couldn't remember much after that. The incisions ran deep until my notion of vision blurred into the specter of his fiendish grin. Thread weaved its way through me, pricking without mercy. He was right. I wouldn't have to worry about missing my friends. Now, the four of us would always be together in stitches.

THE HEADLESS KNIGHT OF
AVALON

Black clouds hung over the violent waters as bolts danced through the night. I was caught at the height of a raging storm as I traversed the sea in my wooden boat. I could feel the misty waters crashing against my face as I pushed through the crashing waves.

This is it, isn't it?

With a furious grunt, I paddled toward a small corner of calm waters. I moved to the other side of my boat and took a seat under my lantern post guiding the way. Against the still thrashing waves, I pulled a map from the storage compartment underneath the seat.

Water splashed across the image, but I could still see the direction toward an island where a banished knight was said to dwell.

The path to Avalon.

I remembered the exchange I had recently. I was by the wharf, sprinting in either direction under the rain in search of the nearest sailor.

***

"Excuse me, sir." I approached a burly figure in a yellow jacket and a hat. He groaned before turning the other way.

"Are there still any ships available at this hour?" I reached out my hand, but he turned around.

Another sailor approached me from behind. His touch on my shoulder startled me.

"All the docks are closed this evening. There's a storm, if you can't tell."

I took a deep breath and looked out at the vicious seas and the island illuminating a bright orange in the distance. I gritted my teeth.

"It's for research. There's a story of a man who was beheaded and exiled to that island."

"So what?"

The man faced me with an unimpressed glare. He towered over me by several inches. I gulped and met his eyes.

"So, it's said he's still alive—a man walking without a head. I must see it for myself. Please. You have to take me."

The sailor paused for a moment. I shook with each moment he was silent. He began with a smirk and shook his head.

"A headless man living on an island? That sounds like a children's fable."

"I'm certain it could be true. I read sightings of"—

The sailor wasn't interested. He shoved me toward the ground where I landed in a puddle, scraping my hands.

"You're delusional. A grown man should know the difference between what's real and what's not."

"But it could be real," I told him. My blood began to boil at that point.

"You're one of those witch doctors, aren't you?" The sailor scoffed and kicked a pile of dirt toward my face. "Get over yourself. There are no headless men walking around some deserted island, and there's no one willing to take you there in the middle of a storm so you can live out this childish fantasy."

I brimmed with anger. I would not let him impede my research or make a mockery of it. I rose to my feet and rushed toward the line of paddle boats secured against the wharf.

"Hey, get back here!"

I never looked back, even as he and many others chased me. Low on time and fighting the waves, I untied the boat from the ropes tethering it to the shore. I proceeded to paddle off the wharf, bound for the island of Avalon. I never once lost sight of the map I'd brought with me.

I was almost a mile from the shore now. I could hardly see anything behind me—no sailors and certainly no other boats; I may have well been floating in a turbulent galaxy with mere flickering lights to illuminate my abyss. Had I not found the map when I did, buried under a sea of old texts, I wouldn't have made the journey. After all, I couldn't swim.

The waves continued to batter my boat from every direction. I could hear the creaking wood giving in. Still, my desire to see the headless knight of Avalon triumphed over my fears.

I paddled further, doing all I could to keep from capsizing. My muscles ached even as a handful of miles still awaited me. I then heard what sounded like singing—a calling from inside the storm.

The sultry tune pulled at my heart with greater force than any wave, reeling me closer and closer. I paddled even harder, moving sideways much of the time until I came across several rocks protruding from the water.

I was astonished by what sat upon them: women with the lower bodies of fish. Their hair sparkled in a variety of shades from the saltwater. Seashells glistened from the breasts of the singing females—a harmonious aquatic choir I couldn't ignore.

Their mischievous eyes met with mine as I approached them. So enticing. Too irrefutable amidst sheer isolation and shadows. Their singing ended when they saw me paddle into their boulder-crafted nest.

"Well, who do we have here?" one with pink hair asked.

"He looks quite delicious," a blonde one added.

The others nodded with growing smiles. I gulped at their numbers. The song was over, but the allure was still there.

"You're all sirens, aren't you? Women of the sea who drown men such as me?"

"We prefer being called mermaids," one with seaweed-colored hair said.

"Everything else you said was certainly true," one with sky-blue hair began. "Though we don't just drown them. We eat them, too."

"...among other even more nefarious things," the pink-haired one added.

They leaned forward with baleful eyes and swayed their hips in my direction. My heart pounded with the threat they forced on me. Still, something kept me from turning back. I was worried everything else I'd heard regarding them was true.

"It seems you've caught me," I said. "That song of yours was every bit as enchanting as the books described."

"Oh, how cute. You learned about us in a book," the blonde one said.

"Humans are just so fascinating. I can't get enough of them," a red-haired one said, salivating as she spoke.

"Now that I'm here, what do you intend to do with me?" I asked them.

"Were you not listening before?" the pink-haired one asked. "Sailors like yourselves used to spear us down for our scales and nearly hunted us into extinction. As punishment, you'll experience our cruelty however we see fit."

I trembled at the vicious glare in her eyes. There was an unfathomable truth in her words. I knew they were slaughtered by fishermen in many folktales. Some were even forced to shed their scales out of survival and perish in sea foam.

I needed to find a way out of the mermaid's nest, and fast. I had no clue how to trick such a creature, however. There were no stories of sailors overcoming their songs. Worst of all, I still had an island to see.

I took a deep breath and nodded. "I suppose you wouldn't care to hear a story before we begin."

"A story?" a purple-haired one asked. She and the others laughed with amusement. "I don't suppose we do."

"Are you sure?" I pressed with a smile. "It's a rather captivating one. Perhaps even more so than your song."

They went silent. The pink-haired mermaid raised an eyebrow of suspicion. "Is that right, human?"

"Yes," I said with hesitation.

This was the first step in my escape plan. I hadn't any idea if it would work; I could only hope they were as enticed as I was when I first read it. My fingers twitched against the paddle as they stared down at me. My desperation to escape was growing more immense.

"Make haste with it, human. We're hungry," the blonde one said.

They flashed their jagged teeth at me, and rime formed around my veins at the sight. I screamed as a vicious wave came to my left, nearly capsizing me. I tossed my weight against it and regained my balance. Only barely.

I looked back at the mermaids awaiting my story and took a deep breath. I simply recalled what I'd just learned and recited it.

"Legend tells of a valiant knight that disappeared long ago for angering the king of his land."

The mermaids looked at me with skepticism. I could tell

they were losing interest fast, which meant my time was running low.

"As punishment for his constant tricks and remarks against royalty, they had his head chopped clean off, and he was exiled to an island known as Avalon."

"You're referring to that island a few miles from here?" the green-haired mermaid asked.

"Yes." My face glowed with relief as I nodded. "And some say he isn't dead. That he still wanders the sandy surface of Avalon, plotting his revenge against the king that had him beheaded."

I finished my story and was met with the last thing I wanted: total silence. My breathing became heavy. Rained poured over my head as I waited.

"It's a pretty interesting story, right? Perhaps there's some truth to it," one with orange hair said.

"And we do love a good tale of revenge," spoke a red-haired mermaid.

Catharsis enveloped me. I'd stricken the chord I needed to. Rather, that's what I convinced myself I'd done.

The mermaids stared for another moment before turning toward each other. They curled back their lips into smiles and burst into laughter. I was bewildered, unsure what this reaction would warrant for me. Humor wasn't my intention. The mermaids then turned their attention back to me.

"No, I don't think there was any truth to that tale," the pink-haired mermaid said. "Though I'd like it to be."

"Here's a story that is true," a brunette mermaid began. "Would you like to hear it?"

I could only nod, pale with dread.

"It starts with a very handsome man that sailed into a nest of mermaids. He begged for his life. In the end, he was raped, drowned, and devoured for treating our kind like a commodity," the blue-haired one said.

"I swear I've never done such a thing," I pleaded with all I had. "I'm merely a doctor. I conduct research—"

I could tell by the murderous gazes that they'd made up their minds. They had no intentions of letting me go. I stepped back on my boat, taking the map with me. It crinkled under my shivering grasp as I searched for another way out. Any way at all would do.

"You can't escape our call," the pink-haired one said.

They released their talons almost the length of their faces. I shuffled back at the sight of them and nearly went overboard. The flame in my lantern went out, and with the darkness it brought, the dozens of sirens surrounding me pounced.

My ship was soon infested with them, reaching their jagged nails at my body and tearing at my clothes.

"I can't wait to taste you!" the pink-haired one screamed.

I screamed just as loudly, attempting to push them back. There were too many and their oceanic eyes were too hypnotic to look away from.

"You can't do this." Desperation had stricken my core. I hadn't the strength to fight them off. I hoped there was something I could say or do to save myself from their coiling bind. "I need to see if this headless knight truly walks."

"Even you won't be walking when this is over!" the red-haired one shouted.

I could feel the boat's wood cracking under the weight even faster than it could sink. Soon, the water climbed around my ankles, reaching higher until I plummeted into the ocean's lethal embrace.

I flailed my arms, screaming in hopes that someone else foolish enough to traverse the sea in this storm could come to my rescue. As far as I could see or hear, there wasn't. The mermaids continued to rip at my clothes. I was losing track of the slime-covered hands wrapping around me, reaching for where I didn't desire. Suddenly, a tugging against both my legs slipped me out of their coiling hold.

I was pulled into the restless sea. My widened eyes flashed in a panic, searching for what had taken me. I could hear the mermaids' muffled screams as they searched for me, but I couldn't see a face; just a vague patch of orange across from me, seemingly grinning back as my consciousness withered.

I woke up on the shore of an island. I was garbed in clothes that weren't mine, and a fire roared beside me.

I looked up at the sky. The storm appeared to have subsided. A great deal must have passed, as the waters sat rather calmly.

"Where the hell am I?" was all I could think to say. I found trees hanging over my head and a cave to my left, glowing brighter as footsteps echoed.

I rose to my feet and grabbed the nearest stick, lighting it with the flame before me. I held it in both hands like a sword as the stranger's reflection appeared.

Stepping out from the cave was a man with an iron helmet and pieces of armor. He looked at me with a blank stare before breaking into a smile.

"I see you're finally up."

He dropped his armor by the nearest rock and approached me. I pointed my weapon at him and backed off.

"Easy there, my friend." He took the stick by the flame, maintaining the smile on his face. "I'm not here to hurt you."

I stared down at his hand. The heat emanating from the stick didn't seem to bother him. I looked at his orange hair and recognized it as what I saw underwater.

"You're the one that saved me, aren't you?"

"I sure am," he told me. "You still look rather beaten up. How about we warm up around the fire, and I tend to your wounds?"

"My wounds?"

I'd only just realized how badly I'd been scratched by the sirens. All across my arms were quarter-inch gashes into my flesh. I was certain I could find these same wounds elsewhere on my body.

"That sounds like a great idea."

The man smiled at me, and we did as he suggested. He placed my stick into the fire and rummaged through a bag of necessary provisions. After a moment of sharp stings and tightly round bandages, I was taken care of.

"How does that feel?" He wrapped a foot and a half of gauze around my arm with a sticky blue substance coated in the inside.

"Better," I replied with a baffled stare. "What exactly was that you applied to my arm?"

"It's a special remedy," he replied, "made from materials one can only find on this island."

"Really?" My eyes lit up with enthusiasm.

"You seem rather interested in medicine. Are you a specialist, as well?"

"Yes, I'm a witch doctor. I specialize in the various supernatural creatures that share this world with humans."

"Is that right?" He looked back at me with a smile. "There are many illnesses out there humans can't heal with their own reserves."

"That's why I do what I do. I hope that by studying and working beside these beings, I'll be able to adopt some of their practices and use them to cure humanity of some of its most devastating diseases. Perhaps even the plague!"

"You're very ambitious," he told me with a bellowing laugh. "You should know, though, the beings you refer to don't like to be called supernatural. They're just like you, really."

"I see. I didn't know that," I told him with an apologetic stare. "I take it, then, you've worked with a few."

"Oh, just a few." He grinned. "Those pesky mermaids to start."

"I almost forgot. How were you able to get past them and save me like that? I've never read of anyone accomplishing such a feat."

"Not everything that's told gets written down, you know?"

He looked at me with an intoxicating mischievous smile. The smoke filled the air as I nodded along.

"It seems rather fair to assume your experience with creatures outside of humans is rather limited."

"Non-existent, if I'm being honest," I replied. "As I'm sure you know, the practice is considered taboo among other humans."

"Oh, yes. I'm well aware."

"In the end, I only have my fascination and my undying hope."

"Yes, hope is good." He took the pail of water beside him and poured it over the fire. "But it isn't everything."

The island went completely dark. I had no idea what he'd done or why. I was growing wary as seconds felt like an eternity. Then, a glowing ember appeared, illuminating his face and mine. It came not from the fire circle, but from his hand. It hovered over his palm as a single giant flame.

I marveled at the sight. I'd only ever heard stories of people carrying such a power, and I quickly realized he wasn't human.

"Correct me if I'm wrong and perhaps I am, but is that the fire-manifesting ability of a *dullahan*?"

"You know your species well," he replied.

"But wouldn't that mean—"

"That I'd be headless?"

I nodded with shock on my face. With his other hand, he yanked the hair on the back of his head, lifting his head clean off his shoulders. It was incredible. He did it with no effort at all, and where his head once sat was a cross-section blazing with the same orange flames as the one he still held.

He smiled back at me for a moment, presumably taking in my bewilderment before placing his head back on his shoulders like a lid over a boiling pot of tea getting ready to boil.

"What do you think?"

I gulped and took a deep breath. "Well, this is a lot of new information. For one, I thought dullahans lacked heads."

"You mean you thought we lost them?" he asked with a laugh.

"Well, not exactly," I replied with reluctance. As I pondered his question, I actually didn't know. It never crossed my mind.

"Dullahans are born with heads just like humans. The difference is we can survive even if someone were to remove them."

He demonstrated for me again. I was just as enthralled as before, taking in the fires contained inside.

"And does such a quality serve you any purpose?" I asked him.

"Aside from scaring mermaids off, it allows me to store energy in the form of our flames."

"Like the one over your shoulders?" My eyes widened with immense fascination. Never have I read anything of this sort.

"Yes, our heads and bodies are like capsules keeping our fires inside. Of course, we can use our powers as we please."

He tossed his flame into his other hand and tossed it back again and again, faster with each toss as my eyes tried to keep up. He then tossed it toward me. My heart skipped a beat, and I went pale as him before he quickly caught the flame with a laugh.

"That was pretty close, wasn't it?" he asked. "You almost died for a second time tonight."

"Yes, how lucky for me," I said with a groan.

"I was just joking."

I took a deep breath and nodded when I remembered the reason I ventured across the sea and risked my safety. I locked gazes with him while reaching for my map in my pocket.

"Something wrong?" he asked me. "And what's that you have there?"

"It's a map of Avalon," I replied. I pulled out the parchment scroll and flattened it across my knees for him to see. "Legend tells of a headless knight that was sent here—"

"Oh, you mean me?"

His nonchalance struck me. In truth, I shouldn't have been surprised. Those without heads were uncommon, even among the paranormal.

"You're the headless knight I was looking for?"

"You found me," he said with a laugh. "Just don't let the king know I'm still around. I'm sort of trying to avoid him."

I let out a nervous laugh before smiling. This almost felt like a dream. I rose to my feet in amazement. "It's really the knight from legend. And you're a dullahan. How did I not see this?"

"Beats the fuck out of me. I don't even have a head much of the time, yet it all seems rather easy to piece together."

I bit back my amusement as best I could before letting out a laugh. "You're a humorous one, too."

"I didn't get thrown out for behaving, now, did I?"

"I suppose not."

"How about we take a walk around the shore? You could use a good stretching of those limbs after the ravaging you endured."

"Wouldn't that make my wounds worse?" I asked with a perplexed gaze. As a doctor, and someone with common sense, I knew it would.

"Dullahan remedies are different. It's best to exercise your body to fully heal. Trust me."

I still looked back with hesitation. My eyes wandered toward my legs, which were still aching.

"I promise to protect you from the man-eating mermaids."

I looked up at his patient smile. I could only think of how baffled I was to not only find what I was looking for but also learn so much so fast. And with such a friendly face that contradicted all my expectations.

I nodded with a smile, and he mirrored. We made our way toward the shore where we began to circle the island of Avalon.

About a half-hour of trudging through ivory sand and flowing tides passed. We were deep into a conversation I never thought I'd have, especially not with a dullahan.

"So, how long have you been living here on your own?"

"A few hundred years," he replied. "Come to think of it, that king's probably dead."

"Most likely," I said with a nervous laugh.

The dullahan smiled at the thought. "You're rather relaxed, knowing what I am. Are you familiar with dullahan lore at all?"

"I am," I told him with a more serious glare. "I know your kind has a reputation for stalking the soon-to-be dead."

"Yes, we're harbingers of fledgling spirits," he said. "Arriving at the doorstep of those set to die."

"With so many diseases still uncured, you have your work cut out for you." I nodded with a chuckle.

"There are a lot more of us than you'd think. Also, we're pretty easy to spot in the middle of a plague. It'd be like staring into the sea and missing the water."

I nodded as I looked back at the sea. "Thanks again for saving me. I don't think I introduced myself. I feel a bit silly."

"Oh, there's no need for that."

I raised an eyebrow and slowed my walk. His expression didn't seem to change, yet I sensed something wrong.

"And why wouldn't you want to know my name?"

The dullahan stopped in place. He turned toward me with a more sinister glare, illuminated by the glistening moon.

The wind seemed to stand still for a moment of eerie silence. "It's because I already know it."

"How can that be?" I asked, growing increasingly worried. I'd always been rather secretive of my identity, and I was sure, close as we were getting, I hadn't yet told him.

He smiled back and tilted his head somewhat ominously. "Let me ask you this: do you ever wonder how exactly we pick out those who die from the many who survive in the end? It can be obvious, yes. But there's a process."

I began to shake, panting as I gently backed off.

"Where are you going?" He began to pursue me. "I thought we were just talking."

"It isn't my time yet," I told him with a tremble in my voice. "It can't be after you saved me. Not when there are still cures to be found."

"Oh, you won't need to worry about that."

He placed his hands on my shoulders, petrifying me with his embrace and smile.

"You think I saved you out of the goodness of my heart? No. I wanted you for myself." His grin shined through the shadows looming over us, inching toward me. "I'm the harbinger of death, my friend. Only I have the right to decide who lives and who dies."

"Then let me live," I screamed.

"It isn't that simple when your time has come," he told me.

He must have been lying. He had to have been. I couldn't escape his venomous stare, nor ignore the feeling of my energy escaping from me, ripping away through the caustic torment of his growing smile.

"I'm still somewhat of a trickster, you know. Even after death. And as its emissary, I've been tasked with the honor of finding those ready to join me. A simple task for dullahans granted the power to read the names of our most fledgling victims."

Could he really read my name? Could someone's doom truly be prophesied? I wanted nothing of what he spoke of, only to turn back to the safety of my town, where I could at least fend against the diseases. There was no way out of his grasp. Each second, the air grew hotter like an inferno raging toward me.

"Being a witch doctor must be a lot of work—always putting yourself in danger." He tapped his fingers against my shoulders. His touch was as smoldering as his flames. For a moment, I swore I could see my reflection burning away. "All I need to complete my work is a name, and with it, you're mine...forever!"

There was the headless knight disgraced and banished to a lonely island, the creature of legend made of flesh and ember. I realized far too late.

His jaw unfurled and produced a gust of his orange glow. That was the last I could remember. I was swallowed, not by water but by fire. And just as he said, it only took knowing my name to be his, forever in life and after death.

THE DEVIL IN THE
COURTYARD

I t was the night of my big performance. I could hear the crowd chanting in anticipation as I sat before the mirror, applying the final touches to my face paint. My heart swelled with anxiety, and my fingers twitched against the grip of my brush.

Many other performers were rushing to their positions, discussing the logistics of their acts, from last-minute decisions for their routines to how they would celebrate once the show was over.

Can I really do this? I wondered.

I looked into the mirror. I had pale white paint on my face and my eyes were vertically streaked with black diamonds. My lips matched the color, and I had my hair under the belled jester hat.

Will they notice?

A soft pattering loudened into footsteps behind me. I gulped when his fingers tapped my shoulders. Turning toward him, I faced a short man, about four feet, with green and white hair. He had red eyes and a crooked smile.

"What are you still doing here?" he asked.

I took a deep breath. "I'm a bit flustered, is all. I'm not sure I have all my tricks mastered yet."

"Just put on a smile, and they'll love it. That should be easy enough for a clown."

I nodded. He made a point—I had a smile painted over my mouth, after all. I forced myself into a smile, and he grinned back.

"That's the spirit. Now, get ready because you're our opening act," he said before walking away.

I clipped the buttons over my puffy striped attire before proceeding toward the stage. A tiny beast statue with twisted horns sitting on a desk to my right suddenly stole my attention. As if my hand had developed a mind of its own, it stretched toward the purple glow of the statue. Then another hand grabbed mine.

"I wouldn't do that."

It was the man who spoke to me before.

"He doesn't like it when you touch his things," he added.

I gulped at the sight of his more stoic glare. Still, my intrigue in the item wrestled against my will to heed his warning.

"The boss, you mean?"

"Yes, and I'd recommend staying off his bad side. Those that don't typically don't get an encore, if you know what I'm saying."

I could tell he was serious, but why would anyone carry around such a peculiar trinket? I glanced around the changing room, and all eyes veered from mine. The faces of the performers were painted in fear under the paint.

I snuck another quick look at the statue. *Perhaps it's a good luck charm. Would he be willing to share?*

"Alright, I think that's enough chatting for now. Just get your ass on stage and be sure to knock them dead," the man told me.

I nodded and rose from my seat. I took another deep breath to forge the resistance I needed to ignore the statue's beckoning glow. Fascinated as I was, I had a performance to start. I grabbed my pins and my unicycle before exiting the tarp door, where the chanting audience waited for me.

I was met with an audience of over three thousand masked patrons packed in colorful circus tents. Why they'd conceal themselves was a mystery. Still, they were enthralled when I arrived; many even rose from their seats as I walked toward the center.

My racing heart alleviated. I felt I could do anything. I placed my feet over the unicycle's peddles and balanced myself on it. I then began to juggle the three pins in my hands.

The crowd cheered even louder. I didn't have to hide behind the painted smile; I was smiling right with them.

They really love it, I thought.

I wasn't sure if I had what it took to make it; I'd only joined a few days before, and my training was minimal. I suppose I had a hidden talent.

Why are they wearing masks? I thought. *Hiding your face is our job, not theirs.*

With my last pin hurled high toward the ceiling and caught cleanly, I hopped off my unicycle and bowed to mark the end of my performance. I was met with an unexpected standing ovation. I didn't know what was so impressive about my performance. I brushed it off as I made my way back to our changing room and kept something else on my mind—that purple trinket.

I made my best effort to keep my distance from the statue to avoid upsetting any of the other performers. I peered from under the archway to watch the night go on. The man who spoke to me earlier patted my back.

"Great job, kid. We're lucky to have a fiend like you willing to do the dirty work."

"And with such little pay," a tiny, red-skinned female on wings said with a smile as she hovered over my shoulders.

"Of course. You have to start somewhere."

They all nodded as they ventured toward the stage for their performances. I took a sigh of relief.

No one seems to know yet.

I watched a myriad of performances. Fiends garbed in makeup like mine would throw knives at one another against a clockwise turning wooden board. How anyone would trust enough to latch themselves on and welcome those incoming blades was beyond me.

Gremlins adorned in the same paint swung across the trapeze. They caught one another without missing a beat; fortunate for them because the net beneath them was on fire, smoldering even from where I stood as the smoke thickened.

Imps launched themselves over fifty feet high out of cannons before diving toward the ground. With their wings, they rose right back up and fluttered in pentagram formations, earning roaring applause from the crowd.

That's right. This was no ordinary circus. This act was compiled entirely of demons—well, almost entirely.

Sweat rolled down their horns and smiling faces as they soaked up the applause. I looked up at my jester horns with unnerving eyes as the bells rattled. I had hidden the truth that I wasn't a fiend like they believed; I was merely a human with an immense fascination for demons and all things supernatural.

The audience sustained their wave of applause. Almost drowning in it, I found my eyes wandering toward the little purple statue again; it was just so strange and enticing. My feet began to move without my control. I swore the jeweled red eyes began to stare back at me...talking to me.

"Come to me if that's what you wish. I'll quench your every desire."

My heart nearly skipped a beat at the bellowing croon carrying across the chamber. I immediately recoiled to my original spot. Suddenly, the eyes appeared to dim, and the lulling sensation stopped.

Where did that voice come from? I still couldn't look away as I panted frantically. I had no idea what I just experienced. *Did the statue just speak to me? Is such a thing possible?*

The stage lights dimmed. My attention was brought toward the darkened ring as the crowd fell into silence.

I stepped out just a foot or so. Circular lights swung around the audience, moving closer toward the center until they aligned.

What's going on? I don't remember this being part of my performance.

"Ladies and gentlemen." A male fiend stood on a wooden platform with a smile toward the audience. "I give you the man that made this stupendous evening possible. The devil, himself. Our ringleader!"

The crowd broke into their loudest cheer yet. My eyes widened as someone—or *something*—appeared through a purple fog. The footsteps loudened as the tallest man I'd ever seen entered the center of the tent. He must have been at least eight feet tall. His makeup was more lavish than any I'd seen, with his purple and black hair hanging past his shoulders. He had twisted horns and a crooked grin.

"That's our boss," I mumbled to myself. I looked over my shoulder at the statue again, growing more curious about what its significance to him was. I hoped it would speak to me and answer my many questions, but I was given no response.

I turned my attention back to the ringleader. With the

statue's owner present for the first time since my joining, I was far more curious about him.

He flashed a mesmerizing grin at his audience, so full of lust and an eagerness for pleasure. He was just like the devils I'd studied over the years—towering demons that yearned for ecstasy in flesh.

"How the fuck are we all doing?" he shouted.

The noise of the crowd grew even louder. I swore their voices would have grown sore by this point, yet their cheering only intensified.

"Are we having a good fucking time, my children?"

He was met with unanimous nods and other forms of validation from the audience. I glanced up at him, growing more stupefied.

"Of course, you fucking are. It's my fucking show, after all. The *Cirque Du Macabre*!"

Everyone raised their fists in cheer. I worried they'd be swallowed by their joy. The women appeared to cheer especially loud for him. Many even began unbuttoning their blouses. He brushed his fingers through his hair and winked back with another seductive grin.

"That's fucking right. You didn't come here for the mundane bullshit your suit-and-tie-fucking-wearing colleagues brag about at work. You came for a show filled with fucking demons. And of course, you came here for me, your glorious fucking ringleader."

The crowd erupted in more cheers and laughter. His influence over them was impressive; it was a tightening hold laced in vulgarity and self-confidence. That smile never left him for a second.

"I'm the devil in the details you desire—no, you *deserve*—because you're above the rest of fucking society. You've chosen real fucking entertainment. And for that, you have my utmost loyalty."

Everyone rose from their seats, clapping even louder as he took his bow. Many even tried making their way down the staircases to embrace him and smother him with affection. It took several bodyguards to control even the least eager to rush down into the ringleader's arms. For a moment, I felt my heart wanting to do the same. He was truly the wicked seducer I'd studied brought out of the pages and standing before me.

My eyes glowed under his spell. I wanted more, just like everyone else. Suddenly, I heard a voice behind me. It was aching and whispered, dwelling behind the wall across the chamber's other side.

With a sense of unease that came with solitude inside the chamber, I began to follow the voice.

"Help me. Before he feeds again."

I gulped with dread. His voice sounded in deep pain, and I could hear others whimpering just as he did as I approached. Unable to hold back my suspense any longer, I pulled the back door open.

Sprawled across the back were dozens of people, mangled and drenched in blood. Their entrails were seeping out and some of their body parts were missing. Their glassy eyes stared back at my trembling face under the night. The few still alive clawed toward me on the ground, dragging what limbs and organs they still had.

"Please hurry," a man said. "Get help. We're running out of time."

This is a fucking massacre, I thought. I couldn't look away, despite failing to comprehend what I was seeing or why it was done.

"Who did this?" I asked.

"It was him."

With his shivering finger, he pointed toward the ring-leader. My eyes widened in utter disbelief.

"That devil? He did this to all of you?" I said.

I spoke louder than I realized. I also may have appeared to be doing so by myself as the other performers returned. When I heard the footsteps, I made the crushing decision of closing the door and briefly ignoring their pleas to avoid arousing suspicion. I rushed back to my seat and began to wash off my makeup.

"That was a nightmare I just saw," I told myself as I patted off the makeup on my left side. I glanced at the silent wall. "I'm sure none of it was real."

I had to convince myself of this lie. Under the guise of something I wasn't, I couldn't afford to draw any unwanted attention.

After around an hour, I was in solitude and still in my jester suit, shaking as I looked down.

"Hey, what's the long face for? And why aren't you changed?"

I looked over my shoulder. The female imp that spoke to me earlier stared at me with a puzzled look.

I shrugged. "I'm just thinking about something else, is all. I'll change a bit later. I'm rather shy."

"Really? You didn't seem like that before," she said.

"I'm pretty good at putting up a front, I guess. It comes with the territory," I said with a nervous laugh.

She tilted her head at me, still a bit taken aback. "Demons rarely have trouble changing in front of one another, male or female."

I gulped. I hadn't any idea of this information and feared it could be my undoing. That I could end up like them.

She rolled her eyes and smiled at me. "Suit yourself. We're all going to get some drinks at the nearby tavern. Join us when you can."

I paused for a moment before sighing with relief; she didn't suspect I was a human, nor did she or anyone else seem to know what I had seen. But did any of them have a clue what laid across the back door?

The demons shuffled their way out of the tent with jolly grins and laughter. I sat in the chamber alone again. I looked around to make certain I was alone.

I can't hear their voices anymore. Did I actually imagine that, or did I miss my chance to save them?

Regardless of what the case was, I couldn't make another move without some sort of understanding or closure.

I opened my drawer to my left and grabbed a black textbook, *Elandor's Bestiary of the Occult*, a text I'd carried everywhere since I was a child. The spine was worn, and the pages were crumbled, but it did what it needed to.

I flipped through the pages, passing by the various fay and giant species before reaching the page depicting devils—tall demons that could seduce men and women with their charm and their wicked eyes.

This was not new information to me at all. None of it was. I stared at the diagram of a female and male devil side by side. Their purple hair was just like his, yet something didn't add up. Why would a species known for seduction be driven to kill?

I began to hear something again behind the back door. My heart pounded with terror as screams filled the air. I could hear limbs being dismembered and the hideous sound of flesh being chewed.

A small part of me wanted to run for my life, hoping I could catch up to my fellow performers and drink away what I'd heard. I couldn't brush this off again. I rose from my seat and crept toward the door, making sure my steps were as silent as they could be as I reached for the tent door.

I peeled it back and saw it for myself—human bodies being ripped to pieces, their innards spilling out onto the bloody grass as a colossal man in the center continued to feast on their remains.

I recognized that grin behind the stains on his face now. It was him. The demonic ringleader. The devil.

I covered my mouth to keep from screaming or vomiting, whichever dared to come first. For a fleeting second, I saw him turn his crimson gaze toward me. The grin he maintained was more than enough proof he had seen me.

I had no choice now. I needed to run fast and far from his hunting ground. I stormed out of the changing room and into the now dim vacant arena with my eyes set on the main entrance.

Sweat rolled down my face. My baggy attire began to weigh me down, and I tripped over my bell-clad shoes and smacked my face against the dirt.

His silhouette lingered over my shoulder, stalking me in the purple mist. He then flashed a chilling grin.

My blood ran as cold, and I could no longer contain my scream as I quickly undressed. I left my clothing behind and rushed to the doorway, breathing heavily as heavy footsteps followed.

I exited the tent out onto a lonely grassy field. The fact that everyone had left didn't serve me in the slightest; it meant there could be no witnesses.

I sensed a glow beside my feet and looked down to find the statue—the devil's demonic trinket staring back at me.

"You can't hide from your wishes."

I was so distraught. *How did the statue even make its way here?* The voice returned to me as a crimson glow emanated from the statue's eyes. I panicked, nearly falling back. I didn't have time to understand any of this. I looked over my shoulder and saw the devil closing the distance. I wanted nothing of this statue; I only hoped to be hidden and to bury this.

I grabbed the statue and ran to the nearest river to my right. Once I felt close enough, I chucked the statue over my shoulder and darted the other way. The sound of it hitting water brought me a glimmer of relief. Hopefully, the devil fishing it out of the boggy depths could slow him down and give me some time to escape.

I sprinted far from any remnants of the circus tent. I followed the dirt trail home, winding up the path until I found the many glowing lanterns of Elandor welcoming me— or so I wanted to believe.

Everyone pointed and shouted at me, disgusted by my appearance. I then realized I wasn't wearing anything other than my undergarments. I didn't even care; I simply rushed through the streets for my life, faster now as guards tried to detain me for public indecency.

"There's no tolerance for such lewd activity here! Get back!" I heard them scream.

I ignored them in my moment of haste. I still had the devil's mist on my trail.

I shoved more people than I cared to admit—many children and elders who were too slow and in my way. I ran until I found myself in the crowded cobblestone courtyard of the city's heart when a familiar glow returned.

My heart sank at the sight of the statue I had dumped in the river. It was inconceivable. How in bloody hell could it have made it here? I was certain I disposed of it.

Townspeople gathered around it. Many leered with curiosity while others stumbled back in dread, believing the item was cursed or a manifestation of evil. Love for all things occult, they were right.

"Don't touch that," I told them. I yanked it from a woman before she could grab it. "You want nothing to do with this statue."

"That isn't a statue."

I went frozen at the sound of his voice. It was far clearer than how the statue spoke. He loomed over me with his shadow.

"It's an idol. A vessel that always keeps an eye on my next meal."

He appeared in a purple mist. The townspeople immediately fled with screams, leaving me alone with him. I dared to turn around and stare at the towering devil. His grin was even more baleful from up close. I could see where the blood and innards had stained it.

"I'll be taking this."

He easily yanked the statue from my hand and swallowed it in his purple mist for me never to find it. I tried to step back, my heart thundering. Before I could, he grabbed me by the neck and squeezed.

"Now, where were you going with it? It's rude to steal."

I could feel essence draining from me as my skin turned blue.

"You ran out while I was feeding. Did you think I'd let you get away with that? And tell all your human friends?"

My eyes widened. The smirk on his face told me he knew.

"You think you could hide from me?"

He lifted me off the ground until I was several inches over his eye level. I flailed nearly three feet off the ground and struggled to break his chokehold with my fingers as tears began to fall.

"I could smell your human blood from a thousand miles away."

He pulled me closer. I could feel wisps of his hot breath against my face as he swung his tongue around his lips. A twisted part of me still wanted them. Was I still under his curse? Was there any way to break it?

"And as for the idol you stole from me, I have to say that was rather fucking naughty. Especially the part where you chucked it into the fucking river. How would you feel if I took something of yours and threw that into the bottomless depths?"

He pressed his lips against my trembling ear to make sure I heard his every word. "Where only I could find it."

His teeth chattered, and my blood ran cold. My body's trembling motions began to slow as my fate sunk in.

He locked eyes with me and smiled. Something looming on his mind, still—a reason he hadn't consumed me yet like the others. I could tell that much.

"You're a witch doctor, aren't you?"

"I wasn't going to hurt you, I swear."

"And yet, you infiltrated my little performance, didn't you?"

His grip tightened around my neck. My skin was now nearly as purple as his hair.

"It's a fool's game to cross paths with a devil, yet it's one so many just can't help but play."

His eyes began to glow. He manifested his idol through a gust of his mist in his other hand and then stared back at me with the idol.

"I suppose it can't be helped when faced with my charm. I'm just hungry in the end, and you're in my courtyard. More importantly for you, the game of jester you played is over, and I'm afraid you've lost."

A violent flash of purple came from the idol's eyes. The next thing I heard was the sound of unhinging jaws that clamped down on me. It was a swift and effective motion. Just as he said, I lost his alluring game, and he was hungry.

THE NECROMANCER'S KIN

The streets erupted with violent shouts. After a long evening of work, I noticed a woman passing by an alleyway stumble upon an atrocious sight. She froze at the sight of carnage drenched in blood that leaked toward her.

Officials and detectives examining the many corpses surrounded the scene at the busy cobblestone intersection.

"Everyone, move back. This is a crime scene!" the chief official said.

The devastated civilians pushed against the law enforcement officials barricading them from the scene. The civilians screamed from the bottom of their lungs, with bloodshot eyes, mourning their beloved victims.

I could hear most of the bloodcurdling screams as I approached the scene. To be witness to such carnage was less than how I hoped to spend my evening. I would have much rather been reading.

The chief took a deep sigh as the officials held the witnesses off. "We're really in the shit now. There must have been at least a hundred reported deaths just tonight."

"We can't be sure they were all from the same killer," the detective beside him said—a narrow man with his eyes locked on the victim's condition. "There are many illnesses still running rampant here in Elandor, especially the vermin plague that killed nearly half the neighboring city."

"And this one's quite severe. Mutilation from the inside makes identifying the victims all the more of a nightmarish ordeal," another official pointed out.

"I'm well aware. It makes cracking this damn case all the more of a bitch," the chief said with a sneer as he took in a puff of his cigar.

One of his subordinates approached him with a hopeful look on his face. "The reinforcement you called for last evening should be arriving now, right?"

The chief groaned. "Yes, the witch doctor."

"Witch doctor, you say?" His subordinate's eyes widened, unaware that my heavy footsteps were approaching.

"That's right. Someone who lives to understand activity like this," the chief replied. "I hate that it has to come down to asking for his help, but what other option do we have? None of our experts can figure out what the hell is going on."

I walked down the streets, climbing over and around the many victims before reaching the chief.

"You called me, correct?"

The chief looked at me and groaned. "Yes, I suppose I did."

"Hold on. That's the witch doctor?"

The detective's eyes traveled up and down my person. I suppose he assumed I wouldn't be wearing my trench coat or that I'd be carrying more equipment; I only had a single book on me that pertained to medicine found in the supernatural world but with empty pages due to lack of research.

I nodded. "Yes, now what is it you called me halfway across town for?"

The chief scowled at me. "Be a little more grateful. You know what a big favor this is to be out in the field, given your line of work."

I sneered at the disrespect, ready to walk away.

"Can you tell us what's going on here? Maybe an indication of how these people died?" one of his subordinates asked.

I took a deep breath against my better judgment. Pests as they all were, I was at least slightly curious about their findings. "That should be simple enough."

I kneeled toward the closest body to get a better look.

"Cut that arrogant attitude," the detective said. "Most of us have been on the case since it opened last month."

"Tell me," I began, "are you aware that their skin is all gone?"

I looked down at the sinew covering their bones and nothing more. All the bodies had the same muscly appearance.

"Are you joking right now?" the chief snapped at me. "Do you think we're total morons?"

I rolled my eyes at him. "Would it make a difference what I think of you? I thought I was here to help you with this case."

"Something a bit more than stating the obvious would help," the chief told me manically.

I nodded and turned toward the hysterical crowd all around. My eyes then met with a body that took the attention of a certain woman. It was crouched on its side, facing me with hollow eye sockets. I heard the woman yell for her son. Just like many, she was certain of the victim's identity.

"How do so many people here know these are their loved ones? Given their conditions, I'd be hard-pressed to tell the difference."

The chief and head detective shared a bewildered look. It was clear this conclusion wasn't so obvious to them.

"Be that as it may, I think when emotional ties are strong enough, you can tell," the detective told me.

"Is that right?" I looked toward the body on my right again as I rose to my feet. I nodded with a smile. "That one's supposed to be her son? It looks like a dog."

The chief looked at me in outrage. "That's someone's child you're talking about?"

"I understand you're a recluse. A pariah that harnesses wicked powers, but have some compassion," the detective shouted.

I groaned and shook my head. "It's your society that made me a pariah. Excuse me if I make fun of you from time to time."

I glanced down at the body before me and kneeled again to inspect the hallowed sockets. I wrapped my finger around to examine the condition and search for any unusual residue.

"This is a rather systematic job. You can't exactly skin a person and pluck their eyes out in a single swing. Whoever did this knew what they wanted and took their time making sure it happened."

"The question is *why*," the chief said.

"Tell me," I said. "Have you cross-compared these bodies to any that have died from fatal illnesses?"

"We haven't," a subordinate said before his chief could. The frustration it brought him gave me a smile.

"Good to know our valuable taxes are being spent on the most thorough examinations modern medicine has to offer," I told him.

The chief and detective both scowled at me.

"I merely jest. It should be evident, even to you, this wasn't a disease."

"We know that," the chief shouted. "That's why we called you. We need your help finding the killer."

"I know you do. And I'm glad you called me. Take a closer look here and you'll see what I mean."

The chief and the detective looked at one another with visible confusion. I could tell they didn't know what I was getting it, but they were desperate, so they shrugged their shoulders and kneeled beside me near the body's head.

I slid my fingers in the sockets again and felt a light shock. I then turned toward their astonished faces.

"As you can see, this wasn't the work of human hands. There are few beings of the supernatural persuasion that can leave electric residue like this behind."

"Which one do you think it is?" the chief asked me.

I smiled. "A breed of undead known as a *lich*."

I could tell by the blank expressions they'd never heard of such a creature. I couldn't blame them; it was an incredibly rare breed after all.

"Essentially, they feed off mortality to fuel their immortality. As for why they left their bodies in such a particular state, they probably wanted to make more trouble for you to solve. With no fingerprints, you hardly have any leads."

The chief and detective looked at one another. Perhaps by their widened stares, they realized I wasn't just mocking them for the sake of it.

"So, you think they knew we'd have trouble telling these bodies apart or deriving evidence?" the detective asked.

"That's most likely why they removed all the skin and eyes. No fingerprints and no eyes to give off the impression of a human corpse. Though, their lack of mana and peculiar features or size wouldn't have me thinking they were anything else. Even if the townspeople weren't still screaming in my damn ear."

"Incredible," the chief said, "you can tell all that just from looking at the body?"

"I dug my fingers in its eye sockets, as well. Did you miss that? If so, I could offer another demonstration," I said with a mischievous grin.

The chief gulped and looked away. "That won't be necessary."

"Just hold on a moment," the head detective demanded of me. I raised an eyebrow with intrigue.

"With such a unique way of killing, surely this lich, as you call it, would know we'd narrow the suspect list down fast. As you said, humans can't—"

"I did say that," I interjected as I rose to my feet, "but no lich would suspect the government's highest authority seeking the help of a witch doctor."

The chief and the detective looked at one another with smiles of relief, seemingly grateful for my efforts. For once, at least.

"Continue your hunt with this information in mind," I concluded. "Search for lightning bolts in strange places. Typically, they appear in a deep shade of green. That should be more than enough to find the lich's trail."

"Thank you so much. We owe you an immense deal for your efforts," the chief said.

"Obviously, you do. I'll mail you my invoice sometime this week." I turned around to head home, where I had a stack of journals waiting for me to read.

As I traversed the mournful streets, I saw something sifting in the alleyway—a lumbering familiar black figure. I couldn't understand why, but I felt I'd encountered this entity in another lifetime. Did such a concept of numerous lives exist? It was an endeavor for another day.

Speaking with those imbecile authorities was so draining

—so numbing to the mind. I envied the state the bodies were left in. At least they didn't have to hear their voices any longer. Even so, a part of me was glad this case wasn't just a farce they couldn't handle out of their utter stupidity. There was something genuinely paranormal about the case, and I was happy to be a part of it even if they didn't much care for me.

I hummed with a smile as I walked down the streets. The panic-induced eyes of victims were of no concern. All I cared for was the knowledge I gained and the lump sum of gold I'd be receiving soon.

As I moved into a secluded to avoid the people, I heard a whimpering on my left. It took me by surprise since I was convinced that I was alone.

The cry came from a broken carriage to my left side. Underneath the back wheels were two little girls.

What are they doing out here? Their family must be worried sick.

I cautiously approached them, but they backed off under the shadows with every step I took.

"I'm not here to hurt you," I said.

They stared blankly at me. I'm sure they had a myriad of reasons for taking haven where they did.

"It isn't safe here." I reached out my hand. "Let me help you find your mommy and daddy."

The two girls looked at one another for a moment. Their vacant stares drew my curiosity. They began to move out from under the carriage and onto their feet. Their appearances immediately took me aback. They had silver hair with bones ornamented like bows. One girl wore hers to her ankles and the other to her shoulders. Their skin was a shade of brown I seldom saw in such northern regions. How did they find their way here, of all places? My interest was certainly piqued.

"We don't have a mommy and daddy," the girl on the left told me.

"We live alone," the other one added.

I raised an eyebrow. Surely, this wasn't true. They must have gotten upset with them and ran off. That or the far more likely possibility that their parents were dead.

I took a deep breath. "You're too young to be on your own." Already seeping with regret, I took them both by the hand.

"Where are you taking us?" they asked.

"To a nearby shelter."

"We're not dogs," they exclaimed unanimously.

I looked at their flustered glares over my shoulder. "You two certainly like to talk in unison. I take it you're twins."

They smiled and nodded.

"I'll take you to an orphanage, then. How does that sound?"

Their faces sank even lower. I stared in bewilderment for a moment. Trying my best to be sensitive to their needs, I considered the poor reputation of the city's orphanage. There were weekly cases of children being abused in egregious ways I dare not speak of. Perhaps they'd been in this city for quite some time and knew the rumors or had learned of the facility's unsavory reputation the hard way.

I nodded. "You girls can come with me, then. Just for the night."

Their faces lit up as I told them. They nodded and tugged on my hand as they tried to lead me in a direction I didn't know.

"My home's this way."

I turned the other way around. The two of them skipped by my side, smiling, and humming the tune I hummed moments ago.

My head was on the verge of collapsing in on itself. What was I doing? *I'm not fit to take care of children. I dislike humans of all ages. What's worse is the town already loathes me. If they were to see me accompanying two small girls, they'd immediately get the wrong idea, and my gold would be revoked.*

I looked over my shoulder at the decrepit building with broken windows and bloodstains.

I'm the adult here, I thought. *I should just take them to the orphanage, even if they cry about it. A shelter would probably do the trick, too.*

I looked down at their faces; they were so filled with joy at the thought of me taking them in. I hadn't smiled like that since I discovered the occult for the first time. I envied them. I didn't want to let that feeling go, even if it wasn't mine anymore.

"I hope you girls like bedtime stories. I have many."

"Can we also have hot chocolate?" the girl on my left asked.

"And ice cream?" the girl on my right asked.

"I have neither," I said, to which they groaned. "That reminds me. I don't know your names."

The girls looked at me like I'd asked them to explain the case I just solved. They hadn't a clue what I said, it seemed.

"We want ice cream," the girl repeated.

"And hot chocolate," the girl on my left insisted with another tugging.

I took a deep breath before letting out another groan. *Humanity is such a pain in my ass. Oh, well. I'm a part of it. That's how it goes.*

One of the most aggravating hours of my life passed, scavenging the few open bazaars open for ice cream and hot chocolate in the aristocratic neighborhoods during a city-wide investigation. Never for a moment did the two of them stop hopping. Judging by the mischievous grins, they enjoyed making me upset. As the night went on, we found ourselves in my home, gathered around my circular study table as I read them one of my favorite childhood fairytales.

"...and that was the end for little Hansel and Gretel when they walked inside the old witch's home. They were cooked alive and eaten."

I closed the book and laid it across the table.

"What did you think?"

They looked at me with disgust, and I couldn't fathom why.

"That was shit," the girl with the ice cream said.

I scoffed at her audacity. Who her parents were to teach her that language, I didn't know. I was just glad they weren't around.

"Watch that tongue of yours, Ice Cream. Otherwise, I'll toss you out on the street."

"My name isn't Ice Cream," she insisted.

"You wouldn't tell me your name," I said with gritted teeth. "So, that's what you'll be called."

"You're sort of a weirdo. I bet you don't have any friends," the girl with the hot chocolate said.

I rolled my eyes. "Not that I can remember making."

I suddenly felt a sharp pain in my head and an image of horns flashed amidst shadows before vanishing.

I clenched my fists. "What do I keep seeing?"

The two girls looked at me with a puzzled look.

"Are you talking to yourself?" Ice Cream asked. "Is it because my sister's right that you're a loser?"

"I believe we settled on weirdo," I replied.

"Loser's funnier," Hot Chocolate said with a giggle.

I rolled my eyes, feeling the sting more than I expected. The jolt of that image came again. It was far worse. I grunted so loud it frightened them. They quickly cowered behind their chairs.

"Sorry about that. I've just been getting these chronic headaches as of late."

"Is it because you're dumb?" they asked.

I met the response they gave me from my storytelling with the same teeth-gritting disproval. They gulped as they took their seats.

"Sorry."

I sighed. "It's fine. I get these headaches every time I wake up. I'm not sure why."

"You should see a doctor, then," Hot Chocolate said.

"I am a doctor," I said.

Ice Cream opened her mouth, ready to make another sly remark, I was sure. A real doctor, maybe—whatever that meant to her.

"If you say so," she said, instead. For whatever reason, that still hurt.

"It's not so bad. I've had them for as long as I could remember. Lately, they'd just been a bit more severe than I'm used to...and more vivid if that makes any sense."

The image flashed again. I saw the horns and mist. What dark shade it was, I still couldn't make out. My face went utterly pale. The thought petrified me.

The two girls looked at one another before staring back. "Not at all." They shook their heads from left to right.

I snapped out of the crippling sensation and nodded with a smile. "Just as well. Time for you two to go to bed."

"But we're not tired," Ice Cream said.

"That's not my problem."

Hot Chocolate groaned. "Can we at least show you something?"

I raised an eyebrow. What exactly was it they had in mind? What did they think I wanted to see apart from my bed, a book, and a closed door?

"It'll only take a second," Hot Chocolate said.

They looked at me with a different sort of smile. It was... ominous. Were they planning to trick me for the story I told them? Admittedly, I'd been especially short with this rambunctious duo. A story about a wicked witch eating children may have also been in foul taste, but a little respect toward their elders wouldn't have killed them.

I took a deep breath. "Sure. Just make it fast. I have an occult journal waiting for me on my nightstand."

"Occult?" they said. The smile they gave one another left me even more uneasy. I swore I felt a breeze enter my home despite the windows being shut. They grabbed my hand and pulled me toward the center of the room.

"What are you two doing?"

"You're a witch doctor, aren't you?" Ice Cream asked.

My eyes widened. "Yes, but how does a girl your age know of such a practice?"

"This'll only be a second." Hot Chocolate's grin curled across her face.

The two of them stepped back and raised their hands in a mesmerizing fashion that had my heart pounding.

"Just what are you two doing?"

A sudden gust of wind filled my chamber. My notes soared through the air in a vicious tempest as the smiles on the girls' faces grew.

"What's the meaning of this?" I asked. I knew then they weren't human. But what were they? What had I allowed into my house?

From their open palms, beams of green electricity began to convulse. Like plasmic spiderwebs, they swayed and grew.

I had my answer, though I couldn't believe it. I stumbled back in fear, hitting my head against the bookshelf and knocking over a book. I wondered whether the image on the page it flipped to was a coincidence or fate, as a skeletal sorcerer faced me.

"You're liches," I muttered. "You're the ones that killed all those people."

They both smiled as their lightning intensified.

"Maybe we did, and maybe we didn't," Ice Cream said.

"You're not gonna tell," Hot Chocolate added.

They walked toward me. I could feel my heart racing as the blinding rage of their sorcery drew closer, with nowhere for me to go.

"Why do all of this, then?" I began. "Why not kill me in the streets like you did all the others?"

"For one, we wanted yummy treats," Ice Cream said.

"We also thought it would be more amusing if we did this in the place where you felt safest."

My eyes widened. The story of the witch that lured the children to their doom was taking flesh, only it was the children luring me to my doom.

There was no way out as their bolts grew more rampant. They could strike me any second.

"What do you wish to do with me? Wield me as your undead servant?" I asked with a sneer.

"We're not the necromancer you speak of," Ice Cream said.

"We're only the necromancer's kin," Hot Chocolate added.

"What does that mean?" I asked.

"You'll find out," they said in unison, "from six feet under."

It came at me in a flash. Not an image, but a vicious surge of bolts from the twin sorcerers. I'd been fooled. Life was being taken from me, and I'd become another casualty. Six feet under, indeed, I would go.

THE OWL

T he forest whispered gentle tunes through the calm
fall winds. I ventured into the peaceful night in
search of an explanation or proof, perhaps, of a
reported strange sighting in the night sky.

My eyes peered over the web of barren branches, gazing
at the ivory moon—the moon, stars, and pitch-black canvas
were all I could find beyond the fog. Doubts started to settle
in; perhaps I was being swindled by the people of my less
than savory town into believing there was a supernatural
occurrence in these woods. At the same time, I kept up hope
that there could be some truth to the rumors of a castle in
the sky.

I marched through the narrowing trail, hearing the faint
chirps of crickets and the hooting of owls. Something raced
by through the shadows. I made out a grin lurking in the
darkness. Perplexed and rather nervous, as I thought I was
here alone, I pursued this most unusual specter of my vision.

I was fairly certain it caught my stare. It began to move
quicker, leaping over the creeks and ducking under branches.
I moved faster, determined to understand what this entity

was. I ran until we were just ten feet apart, with just a few trees between us, when it paused.

My heart pounded. The creature turned toward me, flashing a haunting smile. From underneath the veil of its ebony silhouette came the face of a man, a most peculiar one with a pinkish face that resembled a rat's. There was a bit too much hair on either side of his face for my comfort. His nose was rather pointed, and his upper teeth protruded.

"Seems you've caught me," he said. "What a tenacious man you must be...stalking the shadows."

I gulped at the sight of his grin. I still hadn't any idea who or even what he was. Was he even human?

"It wasn't my intention to disturb," I said. "I'm chasing a supposed castle hanging in the sky. Perhaps you're here for the same thing and can tell me if there's any truth to the outlandish stories?"

He looked at me and stretched his grin from ear to ear. "Outlandish, indeed."

My eyes sank with disappointment. "Are you telling me I've been led astray?"

"Oh, not at all." He patted me on the shoulder. My skin crawled from the sudden embrace of his bony fingers. "I'm saying there's far more beyond the fog than your eyes would have you believe."

I tilted my head to the right. What was he trying to tell me? What exactly did he know? His attention then turned toward another trail in the distance.

"You'll need to summon it—the castle that floats over these woods."

My eyes widened. I was almost positive he was joking. Just what sort of lunatic had I found in this forest?

"Summon a castle?"

"Yes. To do so requires a rather peculiar ritual and specific ingredients."

I could only imagine manifesting the various spells and incantations I'd studied in the old Miskeritonic library after hours. I didn't believe any of them could be true, yet he spoke with such conviction. And I wanted to see this castle.

"What ingredients would I need?"

He grinned and leaned closer. "You'll need to start with these three herbs found down that path behind me"—I looked toward my left. For whatever reason, the shadows seemed darker and the trees devoid of their essence—"Oleander, hemlock, and lilies of the valley. A large handful of each."

My eyes widened. "You jest? All those plants are poisonous."

"You'll also need the tail of a rat and the eye of a frog. Extract the parts while the animals are still alive. Otherwise, the ritual will fail."

I gulped at the morbidity of this list. I questioned whether I had the stomach to attain what he asked for.

"Lastly, a sharpened stick dipped in the blood of the one performing this ritual. In this case, yours."

My face flushed. There was no veering those stoic red eyes of his. I took a deep breath and nodded.

"You're not tricking me, are you? I perform this ritual and a castle will appear in the sky?"

"That is correct."

"What is? Did you answer my first or second question?"

His only response was a docile chuckle. I looked at the darkened clouds, which somehow appeared clearer, as if sprouting the seeds of my doubt.

"And what do I do once I attain all these ingredients?" I asked.

"Gather them in the meadow eighty paces from where we stand. Place them in a circle and wait for the hoot of the owl. All will be made clear."

"The hoot of an owl?" I raised an eyebrow. "But that isn't" —

He vanished—swallowed into the shadows, leaving me alone with this scavenger hunt.

What he told me wasn't clear at all, nor did it sound possible. One thing he said was true, however; there's more to this world than what lies beyond the fog. For years, I'd studied such occurrences and read about the bizarre creatures that inhabited this land. Perhaps there was more fact than fiction to this ritual.

I took a deep breath and set off on the scavenger hunt, starting with the three pitcher plants.

I walked down the darkened path, gazing at the bushels of plants by every stone and tree. These grounds were more fertile than they would have me believe. The variety of plants was quite impressive, yet also deadly. Nearly every leaf or root by my ankles could kill me if I got too close. I dug into my trench coat for a pair of gloves.

I found the first of the three plants he listed—oleander. Their long and dipping petals were as mesmerizing as they were lethal for those unaware of the plant's touch. I carefully plucked about a dozen and placed them in my knapsack before moving on.

Next was hemlock. Its tiny white petals in clusters hardly drew my attention. I probably walked past a few bushels before finding the one before the rotten tree. These were far from subtle if consumed. I yanked a handful of them before shaking off the shivering sensation I got from being around so much poison.

Last of the plants were lilies of the valley, so dainty and small like teacups. I remember reading of a seductress of the same name that fostered the world's earliest sins. I wondered if her temptation had inspired the emotion these plants would give you. Regardless of my speculation, I needed them for this ritual. I took a dozen of them and stuffed them into my knapsack before leaving this lethal path for the pond up ahead.

I wasn't looking forward to gathering the next few ingredients. However, the bogs were full of croaking frogs. I just needed one of their eyes.

I looked around for the largest one, believing it would be the easiest to keep from slipping and found one perched upon a rock. I took light steps toward it with my hands out, holding my breath.

I was just inches away now, but it still didn't seem to notice me. In that moment, however, I was filled with doubt. I always disliked humans for the way they mocked my fascination with the occult. Animals of all kinds, however, I really liked. They never judged my interests. They never bothered me. This frog was no different, so could I harm it? I couldn't. There was no way. As it turned toward me, I had no choice but to abandon this venture and hope I could grow the wings to fly toward this elusive castle instead.

I heard something in the water a few feet away. I stepped forward to investigate and found a severely injured frog laying on its back. Its guts were pouring out, and it had bite marks burrowed within. It seemed a larger animal—a snapping turtle, perhaps—had attacked it. There were no other creatures around it as it struggled to hold on to life. Its eye would be sufficient for the ritual, and the frog looked as if it would die soon, anyway.

I had to close my eyes, rather selfishly, given what I was taking. I kneeled and wrapped my hands around it. I slid my thumb across its body, feeling for what felt like eyes. Everything was so slimy. I reached for a potential opening and a bulge out of the head. In a swift motion, I plucked what I needed.

I tried to rid myself of this memory. I stormed from the forest in tears and guilt, leaving the frog alone to die.

It was heartbreaking as it was a sobering reminder of my childhood. I'd lost many relatives, my father included, yet their demise never bothered me; nature merely ran its course. No medicine could save them, and that was all. But with this frog, I felt so empty, torn and scavenged like how I treated it.

In my mind, I could see the haunting punishment for my actions reaching out with a purple claw. Fog of the same shade plagued every corner. There came the screams of those I'd lost torn away. I dropped to my knees. What was I supposed to do?

I didn't have to ask myself; I made the wrong decision, and I knew it. A part of me now agreed with the mockery I'd always received. How could I defend something like this with just curiosity? Perhaps I hoped to prove the naysayers wrong in the end. To show them the value that comes with knowledge.

I still had two ingredients to gather. The next was a rat's tail. Hopefully, if I imagined the face of the man I encountered prior and his more human characteristics, I could make gathering this piece easier.

I looked toward the trees for one scurrying across the bark. I could hear squeaking in the distance, loudening amidst the sound of flapping wings.

I walked toward what appeared to be a nest high in the branches where many owls sat inside. I watched the mother owl feed worms to its many kin when the sight of a rat told me she was also hungry.

If the rat would be food in the end, who was I to save it? Just like the frog was likely to be eaten soon, so would the rat. That was the flow of nature; you eat or be eaten. I was merely taking a piece for myself.

I reached for the rat with both hands, hoping for a quick

pull. My attempt got the owl's attention, and we met eyes. It turned into a competition for the vermin, and I couldn't afford to make a mistake.

I held my breath and lunged forward. I grabbed the rat by the tail and body right before the owl swooped for the catch in my hands.

Its wings were so silent, stealthy in the night of the very highest order until the talons were shed.

I was met with a cacophony of rat shrieks and owls' howls as it plucked ceaselessly against my hands to snatch the prey from me. It hurt. Its beak was like a dagger jabbing at my fingers. I couldn't afford to lose the rat and couldn't let the rat die before I took what I needed, either. I had to act fast despite the pain. I yanked the tail off the rat, earning a squeak before I rushed down the trail.

The owl hooted before having to settle for what was left of the rat, vindictively, I imagined.

I wiped my tears caused by another atrocity. Was any of this worth it? I could only hope the floating castle and the secrets within could tell me so.

There was one last ingredient, which I had no problem attaining. I broke a branch from a tree and dug it into my palm. I wasn't told to carve out any specific shape, only to stain it with my blood. Still, most rituals I studied seemed to emphasize a star shape, and I didn't want to fail after how far I'd gone.

I grunted as the stick made contact with my flesh. I bit back the pain and watched my crimson fluid darken the stick's edge. When the star was formed, I took a deep breath. It was over, and the most important part was about to begin.

The rat fellow's instructions specified eighty paces, but I was far from the trail and couldn't even hope to find it. Still, he spoke of a meadow. Surely, it couldn't be that troubling to find.

I traversed the forest, keeping an eye out for any places where the trees began to thin. I walked for about ten minutes, meandering toward the left without realizing it. From there, I saw what I found what I was looking for—an open meadow in the center of the forest shining under the moonlight.

I smiled with relief as I made my way toward it, leaving the forest and taking my place on the flat grass. I sat beside a rock and emptied my bag of the ingredients. I placed them in a ring before me. What the rat-faced man told me to do from this point was still ambitious. My qualms washed away, however, when there came through the cold air the echo of an owl.

It was a low, ominous sound. My heart pounded as my eyes searched for what could have concocted such a noise. Shortly after, the air went silent, and I was alone again. Until I wasn't.

I heard metal clanging over my head. Was I imagining things? I looked up and saw an unbelievable sight manifesting. It broke through the fog, forged from twisting gears and walls like sinew against flesh. It was colossal, reaching several hundred feet across the sky. There it was...the flying castle.

"It worked. It actually worked."

A smile formed on my face as I rose to my feet. I was ready to laugh with excitement at the mysteries that awaited me.

To my left, a figure appeared from the shadows. It was the same rat-faced man. I jumped out of my skin.

"You again?" I spoke in a panicked tone.

He grinned back at me. "Well done. Now, I believe it's time I take you to my master."

"Your master?" My mind was muddled. Just who would a man like him serve?

"Yes, I am merely his apprentice. To find what you're really after, I'll have to take you into the castle, itself."

My eyes widened with shock as I looked toward the moving structure over a hundred feet above my head. "You mean you can fly."

The rat-faced man chuckled and placed his hand on my shoulder again. "No."

Suddenly, our location changed. I felt dizzy, incredibly so, as if I'd been knocked out. I looked around and found myself somewhere else entirely. The interior was lavish with green and black walls and adorned with paintings of royalty. Many of the faces were obscured by shadows and some were clawed out.

"Welcome, my friend," the man told me, "to the living castle."

It was all astonishing. I walked toward the nearest window and realized I was, indeed, standing inside a castle suspended over the ground. I could see the chambers moving against the wind like the limbs of an animal passing through the sky. The things I could learn from such a place, the ways they could benefit humanity, were unfathomable. My fingers itched with elation as I turned around.

"Thank you so much for this. You have no idea how far my gratitude goes for"—

Before I could finish, I was met with the sight of two shadows, the rat-faced man's and another approaching from the dark corridor to my right. It was enormous, far from that of any mortal. I could keep my heart from racing with terror.

"Sir, there's something in the shadows. Move while you can."

The rat-face man grinned and tilted his head. Every aspect of his expression was so unsettling, as if he knew something I could never.

"Oh, don't worry," he said. "That's only my master."

Suddenly, he soared out of the shadows with a manic hoot, beating feathered wings as he pounced on the rat-faced man and began consuming him.

I looked with such dread. My entire body shook as a towering entity dug its teeth deeper into him.

I couldn't speak; I stumbled back, peering toward the window. I wondered if I could survive the landing. I could hear a snicker that took me by surprise. I gazed at the rat-faced man, who kept a smile on his face, even as he was consumed.

"Don't be afraid. This is only human nature. We all eat or get eaten in the end. This was simply my time."

My heart thundered in despair as the ferocious jaws ripped at his face. I recalled something I'd said earlier, but how did he know? Was it him stalking me from the shadows all along?

"This isn't human." I whimpered. "None of it is."

There was nowhere to run, nowhere for me to hide from such an abominable creature. I could only watch as he devoured the rat-faced man, leaving him down to only the bones of his frame.

This creature had a human-like face and cast a shadow of an owl against the castle walls as he snickered with delight. He wiped his mouth before standing upright. I was mortified by his oversized physique.

He rose to an astonishing twelve-foot build with feathered wings connected to his arms and had scaly bird-like legs. His eyes were pure red like blood, and he dressed aristocratically like in the paintings.

Never had I seen or heard of such a creature. Never had I been so terrified at the face staring me down.

He walked toward me on his legs that bent backward. I could hear a faint bellowing hoot with each step he took. He smiled down at me, flashing his blood-stained fangs.

"Now, you must be the witch doctor."

I gulped and nodded. "How did you—and what are you?"

He smiled from ear to ear. "As my meal told you, I'm his master and owner of this castle. You can call me The Owl."

I took a deep breath, yet my heart raced as he leaned forward. I'd heard few cases of anthropomorphic entities, never one like an owl. Never so large.

"Come with me." He reached out his hand. "I have something I'd like you to see."

There was no way I could follow him. No secrets or truths at the end of this nightmare could be worth it.

"I have a few patients I'd like for you to take a look at."

"Patients?" I said out loud without realizing it.

"Yes." He darted forward until his crimson eyes were level with mine. "They're in urgent need of your care. A mortal curious enough to make his way this far wouldn't turn away from an opportunity such as this, would he?"

I could feel something inside me being ripped out as he spoke. His blaring gaze swayed against my soul, burning brighter and turning my inhibitions to stone.

"I suppose I could take a look."

"Excellent. This way."

The Owl proceeded down the path on the left, making ominous strides through the shadows as I followed him, shackled by his gaze.

We walked through a hall that appeared endless. It twisted and turned as its very structure would reconfigure. I glanced at the paintings again, this time with the vacant stare he left behind. I could only notice now just how much blood was splattered across the walls, nor the scratch marks.

We finally reached our destination—or so it seemed. A large door with a curved arch stood before us. I could hear high-pitched hoots from the other side. I hadn't the control over my mind to figure out what it could be; I was still under his spell.

"I'm glad our paths crossed this evening, you know. I was getting worried I'd missed my window of opportunity."

He flung the door open. Inside was a massive chamber of gray silhouettes and the smell of rotting flesh and excrement. There was a single stone path in the center and a steep incline all around. I could feel something was wrong as we walked. The chamber was filled with countless bodies picked to the bones. Leaves and branches were scattered all around, and the echoes of hoots only grew louder. His spell could no longer contain me. My location took hold of me.

"Here, we are."

The Owl walked me to the path's end below which were his patients, a colossal nest filled with infant owls. Each owl was greater than human-size. Their faces were stained with blood and there were skulls scattered in the center.

Fear took hold. I wanted nothing more than to run, and that's exactly what I tried when I felt his claws pulling me back.

"Now, now," he said. "You haven't cured them yet."

"Let me go!" I screamed. I flailed my limbs every which way, sprinting against his grasp. I refused to die here, to meet the same fate his apprentice did. "They aren't sick."

"I never said they were." The Owl chuckled and pulled me closer. "I just said they needed your care."

He grabbed me by the neck and lifted me over eight feet off the ground and dangled me over the nest. My eyes widened at the ravenous horde just under my feet. I was at the total mercy of this monster.

"My children are hungry, you see. And they're very picky eaters." His grip around my neck began to loosen. The owls jumped higher as my shaking legs reached closer. "I'm sure you can understand."

My heart thundered out of control. I tried not to scream. Was there anything I could say? Anything I could do?

The owl leaned forward with a grin. I could feel his fangs just beside my quivering ear.

"It isn't nice to steal an owl's hunt. Those that do get punished, you see."

My eyes widened. He knew. He knew this entire time what I'd done to that mother owl. It mattered not; she still had her meal in the end. Now, so would the nest before me.

"Farewell, little witch doctor."

He unfurled his claws and released me from his grip. I screamed the entire way down as I rapidly approached my fate. Everything went dark faster than I could comprehend. I heard a cacophony of hoots and felt my neck snap. In that moment, nature reared its ferocious head. He was the owl and I the rat.

THE COIN COLLECTOR IN
THE INVADER'S TOMB

I t was another brisk fall evening. The city's bazaars swarmed with customers, a common occurrence that made me avoid this walk most nights—I preferred shopping in the mornings, anyway. However, there was a great deal of construction I had to contend with that had only just been completed. This meant everyone had to wait, leading to the crowding of starving townspeople.

I bobbed around with the wave of people; I suspected some shoving was on purpose.

"Go home, witch doctor!" small children would yell at me.

"Your kind aren't welcome here!" their parents would shout while throwing misshapen produce at me.

That answered my suspicions well enough. Of course, their belligerence didn't stop there. It never did. I closed my eyes and shielded my face from the pelting. Eventually, I escaped through the crowd.

I was rather used to this behavior caused by their blind bigotry and ignorance, spawning a new generation of hate where they could. It was in these moments I wondered why I even bothered doing what I did for them. Why search for cures for their greatest diseases if I was going to be vilified, anyway?

Perhaps it would be best if I let a ravenous plague wipe them all out?

I smiled at the thought as I wiped tomato juice off my face. I knew deep down humanity would thank me in the end.

I proceeded through the streets, glancing at the bazaars and the nasty grimaces of their unwelcoming patrons. The opportunity for food seemed to dwindle; each stand would turn up empty once I reached the front of the line. There was one that seemed opportune with my favorite farm produce.

"Can I get a dozen eggs?"

"Sorry, sir. We're all out."

I looked at the merchant's face, dumbfounded. I could plainly see a crate full of eggs beside his feet.

"Do you take me for a fool?"

"Excuse me?" he asked with a sneer. The gall of this man and his repugnant onion breath!

"You're lying to me. I can see several dozens of eggs just beside you."

He looked to his left, faking innocence, as if he was seeing them for the first time. He then turned toward me again.

"Those are reserved for a very wealthy customer."

My jaw dropped. I scoffed at the sheer stupidity of his claim. "Two things, fat man. One is aristocrats don't eat eggs. Two, you know as well as I that you're not allowed to reserve food for other customers. Bazaars are heavily monitored. It's first-come, first-served. Plain and simple. Now, hand me those fucking eggs."

"They're misshapen."

My eyes flared at him. Every inch of his smirk was asking for it. I didn't care that I'd attracted a crowd. He would not take advantage of me any longer.

"I'll show you misshapen, you grotesque prick!"

I grabbed him by the collar and pulled him over his stand. Everyone gasped as I tossed him to the ground and rammed my foot onto his head.

He looked up at me, shaking in terror. It seemed he was learning his lesson about lying and mistreating me.

"I'll ask you again, sir. Can I please have a dozen of your eggs?"

The man's cowardice turned to disdain. His eyes flared, just as mine earlier did. "You monster!"

Suddenly, several sets of arms grabbed me.

"Unhand me. Do you not see what he just did?"

I watched the merchant escape in one piece. The others who dared comfort him scowled in my direction.

Their hold on me tightened as they began to drag me against the cobblestone.

"Just where the hell are you taking me?"

"Where your kind belongs..." a middle-aged woman told me with a bloodshot gaze. "...in prison."

I stared back at her in shock. What sort of backward fate was I being dealt? She was dimwitted, of course—all these people were—yet how could they unanimously agree that the oaf behind the egg stand was the victim? Because I was a witch doctor?

I peered over my shoulder. I could see the prison they spoke of far off the city's outskirts. It was encased in gray stone walls topped with barbed wire. I'd never once seen anyone enter that facility and escape, not even the guards.

I gritted my teeth. "I'm not going anywhere. You all can eat my shit!"

I kicked the woman holding me and broke her grip on my arm. I punched her across the nose, knocking her over. She screamed in pain, prompting shouts from the others who rushed to her aid. Their distraction gave me the opportunity to start my escape.

I elbowed and punched whoever else I had to, whoever was in my way. I slid through the mob and made my escape, rushing down one of the less occupied paths with immense haste.

"Get that bastard!" I heard a man shout.

"Don't bother," another said. "He's history down the path he's going."

I panted heavily as I ran on. The crowd started to thin, and the stands became scarce. The air also seemed thinner. Foggier. Something was wrong. Perhaps that second man was right.

I moved downhill toward a part of the wharf I'd never ventured into. The boats lining the shore were not government sanctioned; the flags of an unfamiliar nation made that clear enough. Even so, I kept moving. I needed to get away from the real monsters trying to ensnare me, and I was still starving.

A ran for another few minutes, widening the distance and making lots of turns until I felt I'd distanced myself enough from the townspeople. I slowed my pace to take in my surroundings and realized I'd never seen this part of town either.

The number of stands seemed to increase again, despite the stands differing from the ones I left behind. I could not see the food I was after on display. In fact, there was no food at all; the merchants appeared to be selling illegal weaponry only—an assortment of chemicals and explosives.

I was bewildered by it all. I took in the sight of cloaked merchants making their discreet exchanges. Privacy seemed a priority here as the shoppers had masks and collars covering their faces and long coats to shroud their bodies.

I'd ventured into a different world, it seemed. I could feel the miasma of corruption seeping into the air from the distrusting grins turning toward me. Each way I turned was someone aiming to take advantage. I didn't mind their stares; they could look at me all they wanted. They weren't getting a shred of copper from my pockets, at least until I had some food for the evening.

I walked past a few stands selling blades, then another selling deep-sea-hunting equipment I assumed was stolen or used to exhaustion by the rough condition. I settled on a stand where a woman stood behind radioactive waste for sale. It came in transparent tubes of various sizes, from the size of my finger to the size of my body. Why did I choose such a treacherous stand to begin my hunt for dinner? Perhaps the green liquid bubbling within drew me in like an appetizing meal in one's dangerous dream?

I waited behind the three people in line—two women and a man—who didn't pay me any mind. Frightened a bit as I was, this field of nefariousness was beginning to resemble a paradise.

I tried not to smile, especially as I reached the front of the line, where I was certain she wouldn't be shy about her inventory.

"What can I get you, handsome?" the woman behind the stand said. She rolled one of the tubes between her fingers with a smile.

"Well, you see"—

Her appearance took me aback. She had an eyepatch over her left eye and a metal right hand. I wondered what sort of accident she'd had to sustain such horrible injuries.

"I've got some pretty toxic stuff here. It'll melt right through even the thickest of naval ships," she said with a grin.

"I'm sure." I gulped. "Though who would be interested in committing such acts? Do I look like that sort?"

"I'm what you call an expert in all things radioactive," she said. "Just tell me the job you want done, and I'll have a tube tailored to your exact request."

She winked at me and smiled. I couldn't tell if she was being flirtatious or simply a good saleswoman. Either way, she had my attention.

"That's a very enticing offer, but I was wondering if you could point me toward the nearest food stand."

She looked at me with utter disgust. She pulled a dagger from under the stand and drove it just inches from where my hand sat. Much of the market went silent, me included. I looked at her scowl, absolutely pale.

"Are you stupid? Just what do you take me for?"

"I was just asking if you knew of a nearby place to get food. Not that I wouldn't purchase something here."

"Is that right?" She smirked and leaned forward. Her long, flowing orange hair was clearer from out of the shadows. She was far more beautiful than I expected; I found myself staring into her blue eye now—the intact one, of course. "You picked a rather strange place for your market run, don't you think?"

"It was more the other way around. I'm less than welcomed in much of Elandor and, well, I was chased out of the principal market after an altercation."

"Really?" Her eyes lit up. "You sound pretty fun to be around even if you look a little bookish."

"That's because I'm a witch doctor. I mostly just read. If I'm lucky, I examine a few patients—"

"Don't care," she interjected. "If food's what you're looking for, I know of a guy that sells rare coins by the wharf."

I raised an eyebrow.

"What exactly does that have to do with food?"

She rolled her eyes. "You buy food with coins, dumbass. And the rare coins will get you more."

I nodded slowly in agreement. "Fair point."

"And the exchange rate here in the underworld market is incredibly low because we're trying to get rid of this shit fast."

"Underworld market?" I looked around. The title made more than enough sense. "I probably shouldn't ask how you acquired these things then."

"Not unless you want my buddy in the stand beside me to cut you up."

I looked at the towering man behind the next-door stand. He was around seven feet tall and had a thick beard. He brandished different blades between each of his fingers while grinning down at me, seemingly eager to carve me up.

I gulped and nodded. "That won't be necessary. You said this rare-coin collector could be found down by the wharf."

"That's right," she said. "With the stuff he carries, there's no way you'll get chased out of anywhere anytime soon. You'll be dining like a king."

I stopped to imagine the picture she'd painted for me. Naturally, it was enticing. In the end, I wanted to be far from a king.

"Thank you." I turned around and walked toward the wharf, hoping against the fear swelling inside I could find what I needed.

"Hold on," she said.

I turned around. Without warning, she tossed me a green tube of radioactive waste. I gasped it after nearly dropping it on the ground, and the heat registered. She snickered as I bounced it between my hands like a scorching hot potato before just catching it between two fingers.

"You're a slippery one, aren't you? I like that," she said.

"Tell someone when you're throwing acid at them, why don't you?"

She looked at me with a smile—a mischievous one that had me somewhat entranced.

"That tube's on me. Just be sure to return the favor when you're rich."

She undid the top button of her shirt, making her way to the second button as she looked at me with a seductive grin.

I gulped and nervously nodded. "Of course. Thank you for this."

I continued toward the wharf with her gift. I wasn't sure what had me the most frightened—my destination, handling stolen radioactive waste, or the possibility of having to sleep with the merchant in exchange for this and the information. It didn't matter, really, as long as I could shop for my dinner in peace.

I ventured further down the streets where the number of stands grew sparse again. I could feel the misty air hitting my face as I reached the water.

"A rare-coin seller?" I muttered. "By the wharf?"

I couldn't see any stands in sight; only the large ships lined against the wharf. The red and black emblem of a skull left me a bit shaken, but I didn't come this far just to turn around. I took a deep breath and proceeded toward the algae-covered boardwalk patrolled by soldiers.

"I beg your pardon," I said to one of them. He stopped and met me with a pale glare that startled me. He didn't say a word, seemingly waiting for me to speak.

"I was just wondering if you knew anything about a collector of rare coins."

He remained silent. He didn't blink even once as his gaze pierced me.

"I'm not a collector, myself. I simply heard word of a way to get a little extra money for purchasing food. And if certain coins could help me reach the front of the line, all the better. Right?"

I must have sounded like a child abandoned by his

parents. There was no chance this bumbling brute would answer me.

The guard looked over at the other three approaching him from different distances. They all stopped by him and nodded at once.

"You speak of the red giant. Is that right?"

"The what?" I asked.

"Follow where the tides ebb beyond the deepest parts of the shore. There, you'll find what it is you seek."

This bizarre riddle dumbfounded me. He didn't flinch or show any hesitation behind what he spoke of. I was reluctant to ask any more questions. Instead, I turned toward the other guards, and each gave me the same stony expression.

I set off on my mission, looking for what he spoke of—the point where the tides ebbed beyond the deepest parts of the shore...whatever that meant. Hopefully, I could find it soon.

I moved down the boardwalk. Each step creaked under my weight. I feared falling through any moment and plummeting into the sharp rocks the relentless sea crashed against. The further I walked, the fewer the ships became. Soon, they were all behind me. I looked back at the mile I'd walked with discomfort. Why did I continue to find myself on my own? And where exactly would I find myself next?

My eyes wandered amidst the sound of seagulls cawing through the misty air. I was rather sure at this point that the soldier was trying to get rid of me with a well-coordinated lie. I looked toward the tides. They climbed high against the shore, under the full moon. The chance of them receding any time soon was near impossible. Yet, I heard something. The groaning of something large in the water.

My heart paced up. The sea began to retract, ebbing just as the soldier had said, then a door revealed itself across the ocean's surface.

My eyes widened. Was I dreaming? What sort of being could have done something like this? What could control the tides? I then remembered he also spoke of a red giant. Hunger eluded me; it was now my curiosity that needed to be quenched.

I walked until I reached a staircase. I hesitated as I stepped down toward the drying shore. I approached the wooden double door upon the sand, mystified by the sight as I was nervous.

I kneeled to pull the iron ring handles when something on the other side pushed the door open, nearly knocking me over. I watched in horror as something began to appear.

The humanoid creature stood ten feet tall, with wet black hair down to his elbows, long talons, and deep red skin. I immediately knew who I was dealing with, who the rare-coin collector was I'd be meeting.

"You've come far to get here, human. What exactly is it you want?"

I had to step a few feet back as he fully exited what appeared to be an underwater cellar. He towered over me by four feet. It was mesmerizing!

"I've come for rare coins," I said as my teeth gnashed. "Just one, really. I'm hoping I can use what you offer me to purchase some food for this evening."

"You seek such riches in exchange for mere food?" His eyes widened at me, and my face went pale.

"Well, I was thinking if the townspeople saw what I was carrying, they wouldn't give me such a hard time whenever I shopped. A little privilege, you can call it."

The red giant smirked. "You don't want food or coins or privilege."

"I beg your pardon?"

"You want respect."

His tone was suddenly direct and drab, and he was right.

My hands shook as my mind flashed with the faces from back in my city. They hated me out of prejudice and their willing ignorance. I was sick of it. My eyes began to dim as the aggravation brought my blood to a boiling point.

"Is that the sort of thing you could offer me?"

He smiled. "Follow me."

I didn't spare a moment. If he had it, I wanted it. I followed him into the cellar where the doors closed behind us, and the waves returned to submerge the entrance.

We moved down the massive steps of the cellar. I had to hold on to the railing to keep from stumbling. As we moved further down, there came a dim yellow light from what seemed to be a chamber below.

The red giant didn't say another word as we reached the musty floor, nor when we traversed the ashen lair.

There, we were met with a syndicate of various creatures. To my either side were creatures with pointy ears, about three feet in stature with mud-colored skin, mining the walls with pickaxes to fill their carts with rocks of gold.

"Those are my goblins," the red giant told me. "Don't pay them too much attention; they'll assume you're looking to play tricks."

I nodded along with a baffled stare. I had some knowledge about these mischievous creatures but couldn't remember when I learned of them. As I stared, they looked over with grins. Just as they did, the giant turned me in the other direction with a push of his hand.

We continued down the chamber where the ceilings rose higher. The wooden rafters arched over four hundred feet across. They were suspended about a quarter of the distance up.

I noticed a different sort of creature—a few, in fact. Hunched beasts with pointed ears and green skin covered in warts. They stood around fourteen-foot tall, if I had to guess, and smelled worse than the egg merchant. Beside them were even larger bloated beasts with pink skin. Though they resembled the merchant more, they must have stood in at over four feet their senior.

The carts they pushed were minute and far out of proportion for them. The pink ones would even lift the carts over their shoulders.

"The smaller ones are trolls and the larger are ogres. They're dimwitted, but do good work," the red giant told me.

I feel like I'd seen them somewhere, too. Why couldn't I remember? Surely, I'd encountered such entities at the academy. The images of chalkboards and texts blurred the more I struggled to recall.

We continued through the chamber where large silver and bronze rods were carried over the shoulders of several beasts —twenty-five-foot creatures with purple skin, and blue-skinned creatures about ten feet taller. I couldn't look away from the latter, who had two distinct heads operating as a unit. What were they?

"If you're curious, they're orcs and *ettins*," the red giant said. "They're rather difficult to train at first, but they're invaluable to the operation I have down here."

"Right."

I was so entranced by it all—the sight of trolls walking across the rafters with boulders in their hold and ogres replenishing the chandeliers hanging over us with their earwax. It was grotesque, yet clearly coordinated.

As we delved deeper, I saw a beast greater than any other. He couldn't have been under sixty feet. His skin was pitch-black. He was bound in chains, tethered by large iron spheres around his wrists, and had rags wrapped around his body.

"And what is that?" I asked. I'd never seen such a creature before. Never one so gargantuan. It must have been in league with dragons in size.

"That's known as the beast of Crolantor," the red giant told me. "They're a rather rare and troubled breed."

"The beast of..."

I recognized that name but couldn't believe this creature existed. I remembered reading an article about illegal experimentation on giant blood that took place on a land that had long been at war with ours. I assumed it was all political propaganda.

The beast roared under the rag covering his face. He slung his wrists, taking the balls shackled with him, and slammed them against the stone floor. Cracks traveled through several yards of stone on impact. The air filled with smoke, leading me to cough profusely; nearly tumbling over.

The rageful fit sent other creatures fleeing in terror. Others, like the red giant, swarmed the area with electric prods, zapping his ankles until his rampant movements ceased. I looked over at the red giant, another question brewing in my mind.

"And just what are you?"

The red giant looked at me with a grin. I think he could tell I was growing wary of where he and these beasts came from.

"I'm just a drifter. But I believe your kind refer us to as *fomorians*."

My eyes widened. That was the name of the enemy species mentioned in the article, a breed of ruthless giants that would invade lands by building tunnels underground. They'd enslave giants and other creatures to carry out their work. Now it seemed I found myself in the lair of these monsters.

I looked over my shoulder. The rippling impact of the beast of Crolantor's slams brought several cracks across the ceiling, and water poured in faster than the ogres could fill them with wax.

"Oh, dear," the red giant said with a grin. "It looks like we'll be trapped here for a little while. I sure hope they can fix those holes soon."

My heart was pounding; I couldn't swim. I turned toward the exit and nearly lost hope, seeing the vast distance. I figured this was the origin of the illegal goods traded on land, and then I recalled I had one on my person.

I dug into my pocket for the tube of radioactive waste. I thought to use it as leverage to have the fomorian bring me back to the surface before it was too late. However, he appeared to have other plans.

"Tell me," he said. "What are you most afraid of?"

"Excuse me?"

The water began to fill the floor, reaching toward my ankles. The goblins slung themselves toward the rafter and clung to the higher ground.

"I think you heard me before," he spoke sternly.

I gulped, unable to turn away his question as I pondered it. The answer was rather clear in that moment, but images I could not recognize suddenly came to my mind. I saw myself falling and large beaks plucked at me. I then saw a surge of green lightning in my study chamber. Lastly, purple horns arched over me, and I saw an ominous grin.

I shook as the water climbed to my waist. What the hell had I just seen? Why did I feel like I'd seen it before?

I turned toward the fomorian still waiting for my response. I took a deep breath and nodded.

"Drowning," I said.

"Is that your honest answer?"

"Why does it matter?"

The water climbed higher up to my neck. I realized then that I wouldn't be able to stand.

"Because."

He picked me up from the swaying water to his eye level.

The scowl on his face told me I was only trading one danger for another.

"I have a very particular method of giving out my rare coins, you see."

He dug into his pocket and pulled out a pure-gold coin as large as my palm and as thick as my thumb. It had the same emblem as on his flags and had an ancient year inscribed on the bottom. The craftsmanship was so unique. I could tell from the intricate indents far more advanced than any I know were used. A rare coin, indeed. Fit for any king.

"In exchange for my coins, the one who desires them must live out their greatest fear."

I shuddered as his eyes blackened down at me. I could feel the water crashing higher up his legs, reaching mine.

"Let me ask you this in a different way," he said. "Is this truly what you want? Will garnering respect be worth it in the end?"

My eyes widened, doom encircling me. Though I wanted to tell him what I still sought, I knew it wouldn't be worth my greatest fear.

"Don't keep me waiting or I'll decide for you."

The water climbed higher. Even with many more feet below me, my lower half was submerged again. The water broke faster as the other giants paddled away on their rafts, riding out to safety.

I couldn't think of what I wanted. I couldn't stop thinking about what I saw—those purple horns.

I reached for the gold coin without realizing it. Why did I do that just now? The giant's eyes widened, and a malicious grin formed on his face.

"So, it is death you've chosen? Very well."

He snarled at me before tossing me into the water. I tossed and flailed, hoping to maintain some sort of balance but couldn't. He pressed his entire hand against my face, keeping me underwater.

I looked up in terror as he stared with a grin. I didn't have the strength to fight back. It was clear I'd succumb to some sort of force I couldn't comprehend. A vision planted itself in my mind. I could feel my oxygen depleting. Everything around me darkened as my will crumbled.

I had moments left to rescue myself, and it was a sink or swim situation. In the end, I sank, ebbing and flowing toward my underwater grave.

CRIMSON REBIRTH

My mind slipped into the dark depths of a slumber more intense than I'd ever recalled, yet I felt I'd experienced this many times before.

There wasn't a speck of light to break the suffocating darkness. The fledgling warmth I had earlier became a distant memory. I was freezing. Paralyzed.

I soon began to sense something that wasn't there before —or was it?—the immense crushing on my chest pushing me deeper down. What was it? And what was slithering all around me?

I began to hear a swaying motion. The surrounding air moistened. But how? How could I *feel* if this was a dream? I then heard a voice.

"It's time to wake up. Your rebirth has begun."

My eyes shot open. Whatever dream I had ended, and a nightmare replaced it. The first sight I took in was the hollowed face of a corpse staring back at me under a crimson sea.

Panicking, I flailed back and forth as I tried to break free. The surface appeared so far, and there must have been over a dozen corpses stacked on top of me. Death surrounded me.

I was running out of oxygen fast. My eyes flared as I registered the impending terror and questions. How did I even get here? Did someone put me here because they thought I was dead? And what did that voice mean?

Challenging as it was, I had to put my curiosity aside to focus on the urgency of my escape. I pushed against the mound of carnage, trying to claw my way through. Forceful as I was, I could only feel the weight getting worse and my heart being crushed.

Tears fell from my face as my efforts grew futile. Whoever tried to bury me was going to have their way.

Please, I thought, *whatever I've done to you; however my fascination offends you, I can make the change humanity needs.*

My eyes began to close. I couldn't fight back the bodies or their indecipherable whispers in my ears.

"Just give me a chance," I muttered, "and I can make this world better."

The voice was gone. I was surrounded only by the cacophony and the corpses. My eyes closed on their own, and I sank toward the unpromised bottom. Everything became colder.

"You're too late."

My eyes widened. The voice returned. I looked for where it came from. It sounded like a man, deep and rather alluring.

What are you? And what do you mean I'm too late? I thought.

"Your ambitions have failed. What you seek can never be realized where you are." His voice thundered through the sea of blood, sending a ripple. My aching heart raced at a thousand miles and my teeth gritted from his words.

"You don't know that," I exclaimed. "Allow me to escape from this pit and you'll see exactly what I can do!"

The voice chuckled, mocking my predicament as my

limbs flailed. Fury clouded my mind I hardly paid attention to how deep I was sinking. There were only a few corpses around me now, just a red sea turning black.

"If you wish to escape, you'll need to find me in my lair. Only then will you be offered a chance for salvation."

I shook with anger. I hadn't the slightest idea what lair he spoke of or where to find it. Everything was just so dark and heavy.

The voice was gone. I waited another moment, hoping he would return, but he didn't. He only left me the choice to pursue him to his lair.

I turned in either direction, ignoring my slowing heart rate. Only a few bodies were raining down from the shadows above. I looked for what felt like an eternity under more than a mile of blood. Despair was taking hold. I was certain I was being deceived—mocked again.

I noticed a sudden flashing from the distance, a bright crimson through what appeared to be a tunnel. Could that have been what he spoke of? It certainly seemed like a decent place to start, and I couldn't see any other paths.

I still struggled to move under the weight of the resistance and my inability to paddle. Still, I held my breath and fought to propel my way through the sea of blood. I picked what I'd seen others do by the shore of Elandor—tossing my arms forward, one after the other and kicking kick my feet back in unison to move quicker through the sea.

I had never been physically gifted but was incredible at learning from observation—the best, in fact. Though I was still rough around the edges, I was conquering my greatest fear and learning how to swim.

I had a slight smile on my face, even amidst the uncertainly of my life, as I reached closer to the tunnel. I looked down to see where the bottom was before I entered. I couldn't see anything but the shadows.

I swam within an arm's length of the tunnel before finally hoisting myself in. I was relieved, but I stayed cautious. Though I'd escape the bodies and the surroundings were clear, I was still deep underwater, now with a thick layer of stone surrounding me. I tapped my fingers against the rock. It was unexpectedly warm. Could the light have caused that? Regardless, if this tunnel caved in for any reason, I didn't want to be here for a second burial.

I proceeded into the tunnel. It was cramped at about seven feet from top to bottom. With my hands balancing against the ceiling, I could make my way through with somewhat of a walking motion.

After a few minutes of exploration, I found my rhythm as I took heavy strides down the narrow strait to follow the red light.

The voice spoke of a lair. I thought about that more clearly now that I'd found this tunnel. I only hoped I was in the right direction. I was still holding my breath, so I couldn't afford to make a mistake.

I studied the wall to distract myself from my overwhelming dread and noticed purple and pink diamonds growing from them. They were so captivating as my reflection faced me through each one. It was like I'd entered an otherworldly hall of tiny mirrors. Were they also talking to me? It felt that way.

As I traversed deeper into the tunnel, I realized the voices weren't coming from the surrounding walls; they were coming from above. I heard the voices of many men and women in conversation.

My eyes lit up. Could the surface be just above me? A cave beneath the ocean...I'd heard of such creations. From what the archives told me, entire civilizations dwelled in areas like this. Is this where I could find his lair?

As I advanced, I heard giggling and shouting that had my

heart beating out of my chest. As the distance closed, I could make out the cracks of brutal whips and chains slamming against the stone.

I gulped. There were only ten or so feet until I reached the end of the tunnel—a sizeable gap in the ceiling where faint pink shadows swayed.

I tightened my fists and prepared for the worst, though I had no idea what the worst could be. So long as there was air and a way to escape, I could take the chance.

I took my final irrevocable steps before wrapping my hands around either side of the fissure. I pulled myself through, gasping for the first air I'd taken in for what seemed like a lifetime. It was so fresh. So alleviating.

I dragged myself out and washed against the stone surface. My heartbeat relaxed; the pressure against it was gone. I shook with relief. Against the odds of not being able to swim and whatever had tried to smother me, I'd survived. I smiled and then broke into laughter.

Around me, I could hear giggling songs with footsteps drawing closer. A sense of fear filled me.

I looked up and saw a group of humanoid figures walking toward me. They had pink skin, white hair, and black horns, and they were barely dressed—they covered their private regions with silk. The only other thing they wore were distrusting smiles.

"How delightful. Don't you all think?" a female said.

"It looks like the devil reeled in another one for us," a male said with a grin. "And this one looks extra tasty."

"I beg your pardon."

I rose to my feet and looked around. To my terror, I'd found myself in what appeared to be a lascivious dungeon. I noticed naked humans tied and gagged in devices made of wood and stone being viciously penetrated. I had no idea what their arrangement was, but the lustful smiles on their faces told me they didn't mind. The numbers of the humans were in hundreds, all being seduced by this strange, pink-skinned species.

"Just what are all of you?" I asked.

"You mean you can't tell?"

I heard her voice moving through the crowd, along with the clacking of heels. She appeared in a tight black outfit with a cape of the same color. Judging by that piece of clothing and her confident grin, she was their leader.

She leaned forward and placed her left hand on my freezing cheek. The sudden heat had my body turning red.

"You humans are so ignorant of our ways. I must say I'm hurt."

The others nodded with sullen glares. I could feel their sadness pulling at my heartstrings. The color in my eyes dimmed. Surely, I could remember reading of such a species at some point.

"I didn't mean to," I told them. "What I meant was this is unexpected in more ways than one."

"Oh, I like the sound of that." Her eyes widened with elation as she slid her tongue against her finger. "Keep talking."

I gulped and nodded. "I'm what's known by humans as a witch doctor. I study other races to learn of their ways."

"So, you're the well-educated type," another female said.

"That's my absolute favorite," another said.

The two of them approached me from behind and wrapped their arms around my chest. Soon, more pulled in their direction, while their leader still had me in her grasp. My eyes could not break away from her allure.

"You say you study other kinds? Tell me. Have you ever heard of a succubus?"

"A succubus?" My heart skipped a beat. I began to realize what this sensation was chipping at my inhibition, bringing me toward them. "Yes, you're a rare class of demon that feeds off of dreams."

"Off *dirty* dreams."

She grabbed me by the hips and kissed me with incredible force. I could feel my mind falling into her grasp. I was taken elsewhere, into this foggy vision of her seducing me with all her flesh could offer. We were atop one of the wooden floorboards with our faces dripping with saliva while I thrust from behind. I didn't want this euphoric sensation to end. Then, I felt her lips separate from mine.

"Like that one," she told me.

I took a deep breath. The dream was over. I shook from the intensity of what I'd seen. It felt so real, and I wanted more.

"Did you like that?" she asked me. We both knew the answer, but I grew hesitant to say as all the others closed in.

"What's not to like?" I told her. "Your kind is known for their beauty, and you don't disappoint in the slightest."

"Oh, that makes me so happy," she said with a sultry smile. "That makes my friends happy, too."

I could feel the more aggressive touch of a man's hands across my hips. I looked to my right and saw his grinning face looking over at me, winking.

"And you're the male equivalent...an incubus."

"Yes, I am," he whispered.

"Temptation comes in many shades," their leader told me. "Men and women can both feel it and they can do so in different ways. Even if the oppressive society your kind believes in sees, otherwise."

More hands made their way across my body. I soon couldn't differentiate between the dainty touch of a woman and the firmer hold of a man—I think that was the point she was trying to make. I didn't bring myself to mind at all.

"You know, I've read a good deal on all sorts of supernatural beings," I began.

"So, we're supernatural?" She pressed her breasts against me. I could feel the others doing the same around me. My face turned even redder.

"Yes," I squeaked. I cleared my throat as they giggled before starting over. "You're said to lure your prey in by spells laced with aphrodisiacs? Is that right?"

"Luring prey? No, no. We're just having a good time. Aren't we?" She kissed me across the neck, sliding her tongue around my skin. Many of the others did the same as they unbuttoned my clothes.

"I just wanted to say"—I stopped for a moment, jumping when I felt their hands moving under my belt—"that your spells can't reach through the pages of a text."

"What's your point?" she asked, then yanked me hard between the legs. I nearly let out a scream of ecstasy. I could hardly remember what it was.

"Just that you're always depicted as being so beautiful. If you ask me, I don't think you need a spell. Your appearance can already fulfill your needs."

"Aren't you just a smooth talker?" another succubus said before nibbling on my ear.

"I'm just trying to make sense of all this," I said. "By doing so, I can—"

"You need to stop that," the lead succubus pressed my cheeks in her hand. "Relax. This is your moment. The only thing that should be on your mind right now is the number of ways you're going to fuck each and every one of us."

My heart pulsed. I didn't pay any attention to the raw number of vixens around me, male and female alike, only their collective touch arousing me more by the second. I'd never cared for such intimacy, but I enjoyed the meaninglessness of it all. The futility in such orgiastic pleasures. Truly, I was wrong. Her spell was working.

"Think about this, doctor. This chamber's filled with sodden cunts and tight assholes. Can you imagine sliding yourself into each and every single one?" She leaned closer to my ear, rolling her tongue. "Until your desire explodes."

My legs grew weak. They were becoming a ravenous nest from which there was no hope of evasion.

She chuckled as she felt my appendage press between her legs. "You've got a decent piece on you. This will be fun."

Admittedly, it felt that way at first. However, there was something else I'd read regarding this species and its desire to suck its victims dry. It'd be a better way to die, without a doubt. Still, I'd much rather live. I then remembered something their spell nearly had me forgetting. Something they said.

"You mentioned something earlier. A devil," I muttered.

"Oh, you mean our master," their leader said. She coiled her arms in the sea of limbs around me. "He's a bit busy."

"A man, you say?"

Perhaps it was the familiar crushing sensation. The voice I heard in the sea of blood began to echo in my mind. I doubted such a coincidence. From what I knew of devils, they were quite similar to succubi and incubi; they were simply taller and more aggressive.

"Tell me. Where can I find him?"

Their leader's smile began to diminish. She stared back at me with a frustrated sneer.

"You're a greedy one, aren't you? You're about to get smothered in the flesh of over twenty vixens and you're thinking of someone who isn't here?"

She and the others doubled down, stroking and sliding their hands across me until I could only think of them.

"I was drowning," I said before it could slip my mind.

"There was this voice that told me to find him in his lair. I think it came from your master."

She and other others slowly retracted their movements, stepping back and looking at me with expressions of bewilderment.

"You're telling me our master spoke to you?" a succubus said.

"I'm fairly certain it was him, yes. All I know is I need to find whoever it was, so I can escape."

They looked at one another with puzzled eyes. I hoped more than anything they would let me go.

The leader looked back at me with a smile, impressed. "It isn't often he picks out one of our captives for himself like that."

I suppose I should be flattered... I thought with an ever-unnerving sensation.

"But if you claim there was a voice through his crimson lake, then you must have heard it," an incubus told me with a widened expression.

Is that where I was? I thought.

"If the devil is calling you out, don't let us be the ones to stop you," the leader said. "If anything, that would anger him."

My eyes filled with hope. It seemed they believed me and that they would let me escape their dungeon.

"Just promise me this"—she leaned in—"once he's done fucking you, you're going to come back and fuck all of us, too."

I went pale at her words as she kissed my cheek. I tried to envision a scenario where I could come out alive. The spell was broken, but my confidence in taming the chamber still held somewhat among their erotic bodies.

"Well?" she asked as she awaited my response.

I nodded. "I'll do what I can."

"Excellent." She smiled as she patted my cheek, then pointed over my shoulder. "You can find him if you follow that path. There's no chance in hell you'll be able to miss the guy."

"Understood."

I looked around and saw a different tunnel. This one had a purple glow and led upwards.

"Best of luck," she said. "Though I doubt you'll need it."

I hoped she was right. The group waved me off with smiles and blown kisses. I had my eyes locked on the new tunnel before me, and my mind trembled under the ultimate lecher awaiting me on the other side.

I climbed my way up from the two-foot drop and left their chamber devoted to pleasure. I buttoned my clothes as I walked. I could still hear them giggling and talking about me. I then remembered now that my mind was clearer in the presence of other humans. I supposed that was part of the succubus and incubus allure; making you think their lust revolved around only you.

I looked over my shoulder at their smiles fading under the dark purple light. I couldn't help but think about what I wanted to say before. Though vixens like them could wield aphrodisiacs with perfection, could that not also mean they had an innate ability to use remedies that altered a person's state, not just to make them aroused, but perhaps heal them? I wanted to say that before, but their touch was so persuasive.

There was so little I knew of their true powers. Their healing resources were almost on par with elves, perhaps even dryads. Still, they chose to only use their lust. It seemed like such a waste of potential. Yet, I found that decision so fascinating.

I shook my head. My chances of learning were behind me for now. And even if I succumbed to their desires, I could not learn much in the end; they'd only yearn for more. I had to focus on what was ahead: the purple light growing brighter.

As I got closer, I could hear moaning and joyous cackling. My heart pounded. It seemed, already, he was going to live up to his reputation as the master of these vixens. By the sounds of it, one who reveled in that title.

I walked against the walls of the larger circular tunnel, following the dim light until a small chamber with a single throne in the center came into view. Sitting upon it was a man. He had the face of a succubus pressed between his legs. She gargled on his appendage with watery eyes as he moaned. I shook at the sight, slowly moving back when his eyes locked with mine.

"There, you are."

Color left my face when he saw me. I found my feet moving forward on their own. I didn't know how or why I thought I had seen his face before. His purple horns arching over the image of thick mist I couldn't quite recall.

"This'll only take a fucking moment."

He forced her jaws deeper around him. With a grunt and a slight twitch, along with her euphoric swoon, he finished his business with her. It lasted longer than I expected, at least a few minutes. I squirmed in disgust with every second gulping. Her stomach bulged for such an intense release and once he was done, he pulled her by the back of her hair and released himself from his mouth.

I nearly stumbled over at his absurd size. I assumed a man of his eight-foot stature to be large, but he resembled a horse between the legs.

Where the fuck did she put all of that? I wondered as she crawled across the floor with such a satisfied grin and semen spewing from her mouth.

She picked up her clothes and joined the other vixens

lined against the wall. By their still flattened stomachs, I supposed they were waiting their turn.

"Come here now."

I shuddered at his voice. I took a quick glance and remembered what their leader told me. If his intentions were to satisfy his arousal, the decision to turn back was an obvious one. I'd have to find my own way out and I'd rather it be at the hands of his more proportionate servants if death was my only option.

I froze in place, unable to break eye contact as he smiled back at me.

"I'm not going to seduce you, if that's what you're worried about. You came for a fucking way out and I can offer you that."

I was making a deal with the devil himself—I knew that now as I walked toward him. I was just as desperate as he was probably hoping for. I knew enough about him to realize his kind were apex predators for a reason.

Thoughts of what would I have to give up in this arrangement beat against my mind as the air grew thick with the mist of his purple essence. If it wasn't my body, just what did this towering harlot desire from me?

"I'm listening," I stuttered. "If you can bring me back home, then, please. Tell me what I have to do."

The devil grinned at me. He was so seductive. So abhorrent and grotesque without an ounce of shame. He dug into his pocket and reached for a large black die with purple-spotted indents. He held it with two fingers as it began to glow.

"You don't recognize me, do you?"

Was I supposed to know this man? He seemed familiar enough. His vulgarity would be difficult to forget, yet I did.

"That's beside the fucking point. I grow hungry, you see," he said. A chill ran down my spine as he flashed his fangs toward me. "If you're determined to pass this point, you'll have to do so by playing a game."

I gulped. "What sort of game?"

"Take a look at this fucking die here. It's no different from any other, really. Six sides. Capable of landing on just one."

"And what does each of the six sides mean?" I asked.

He chuckled. "You don't understand how fate works, do you? It's not what you know. It's what you'll discover in the end when it's fucking too late."

My eyes widened at the tormenting truth. There was no way of wishing for one number over the other and no reason to hope for a particular outcome out of six. I could only wait until it landed.

"Let's begin."

He tossed the die. It bounced against the stony floor several times. Each clanging was an echo that dug into my pounding heart.

I watched the bounces lessen and the flashing of numbers slow. A number would soon be revealed, and so would be my fate.

It rolled across the edges, flattening toward a decision. Even though I didn't know what awaited me, my life was still on the line, and I needed the right number to get out of this pit. Whichever it was.

It teetered for a moment between two numbers. I held my breath as it slowed to decide on where to drop.

It fell on the number six. I had studied enough to know that could only have meant one thing—the devil would have his way.

All hope sank as he rose from his throne with a look of delight.

"I can't say this was very much of a surprise. I did know your destiny long before you arrived."

"You what?"

In that fit of panic, my mind flashed with the image of horns from before. I began to realize I'd seen him before and that our encounter, however brief, ended with my violent demise.

"You wish to return home, don't you?"

My face sunk as he walked toward me. He wore the same grin from before, but how was any of this possible?

"Why? Why do this if you're the one who killed me?"

He chuckled and placed his hand over my shoulder. "I said I'd take you home, didn't I? That's what happens when the die lands on my number. Your greatest desires are made into a reality."

"I don't want it," I shouted. "Not from you."

"It's too late. Fate's a charitable bitch!" He grabbed me by the neck. I could feel his choking hold intensifying fast. "Just close your eyes."

My resolve faded. I couldn't fight back his flashing gaze. Everything was growing dark once more.

This embrace with the shadows was more short-lived than the prior. I found myself back where this began—in the sea of blood and hollow corpses, this time, with the devil's face looking at me from above.

I swung my arms and legs in terror, screaming and taking in the blood. I was so confused. More images appeared—of me drowning in a strange mining shaft, around colossal figures, particularly, one with a red face grinning at me.

What was all that just now? What the fuck is going on?!

The vision left me with a throbbing headache worse than usual. None of that mattered. Not now.

The face I saw and that flood around us faded, swallowed by the gaze of the devil and his sea of blood taking over.

"I don't get it. You said I was being taken home."

I never should have accepted his deal. I should have let

his servants do as they pleased. Now, I was utterly at his mercy.

"This is your home," the devil told me. I shook with fear. He floated toward me, sifting through blood. His essence stained the very ocean with his mystifying shade of purple.

"You're lying," I screamed.

"I never lie. What you see here is no sea of blood; it's a graveyard, and these people have long passed."

He drew closer until his eyes were just inches away, and his hand began to wrap around my face.

"This is your home now. Your crimson rebirth."

He was right. There was absolutely no way out either. He knew my destiny this entire time. In a quick motion at the hips, it was over. His talons slashed through the sea, and I was severed, cut clean in half. I was fated to sink just like the others—a rebirth disposed for his deeds.

THE FAY MOTHER

I t was a brisk and gentle evening. The winds caressed my face as I walked through the open field. I could hear the songs of hummingbirds as they flew beside me while the fireflies illuminated the way.

I felt good—maybe it was because I was miles away from Elandor, where I was often ridiculed for my job or because the soft air was relieving me of my chronic headaches.

After many years of taking odd tasks during the day and saving all the silver I had, I could finally afford to venture out to a land on the continent's end where the fay kingdom lay.

I could see it approaching. The towering trees of many species lining the forest's mouth where bulbs lit with a mystifying substance hung from the branches, calling out to me.

Although I needed a vacation from the tediousness of my fellow humans, I came here for a rather specific purpose in mind. Rumor had it that elves were excellent at weaving thread and that the fay kingdom was the place to find the best of it. I had no particular use for it in mind, perhaps to sew the holes in my favorite shirts. I simply wanted to marvel at the craft and be among a kind so fantastical.

I approached the foot of the fay kingdom. In the center was a tree taller than the others, at least five hundred feet, with candles growing out of every branch. Each glowed a different shade.

I heard whispers as I entered. Was it the trees? Was I hearing those that lived inside the forest?

I walked through the expansive archway carved into the tree. Even the interior was adorned with the glowing markings of what I read to be the native fay tongue. I wondered if I could decipher any of the elegant curls and sways.

I soon passed the tunnel and entering a place more magnificent than any Elandor could offer. The skies were filled with a nest of illuminated branches, not with candles but with orbs that appeared to be hovering on their own.

Entire structures were carved into the trees, large yurts growing out of their sides and many staircases connecting it all into a vast syndicate. The air with intoxicating. I could smell so many intense and challenging aromas native to their kind. I looked around and saw many species living here—not just the elves—bustling on the platforms above and the bazaars on the ground.

I dug into my knapsack and reached for a textbook as I walked. I flipped to the portion depicting the various fay. There were little ones the size of my hand known as sprites. They had butterfly wings beating as they soared past my ear. They brought me such a warm smile. How could something so cheerful not?

Some fairies were the most prominent flying fay. They ascended over the bazaars with jars of herbs, dropping them off at the doorsteps of homes; never shattering a single container. Some took in the scent for themselves as they perched over the branches, conversing and keeping jovial grins.

There were others—the more lascivious variant known

as the pixie. I could see them attempting to seduce the male and female elves with wicked grins and especially potent aromatics that nearly had me drawn. There was also the dark and twisted nixie that used black magic and manifested shadows and fire, great explosions of dark rainbow glitter. Some of these fay brought with them applause; others, trouble. In the end, all of them laughed just the same.

I was so enthralled by it all. Tales of fay were my absolute favorite, growing up. I couldn't wait to speak to one myself.

I walked toward the bazaars where it seemed I'd caught the attention of a young female elf. I soon locked eyes with her. She had cream-colored skin and shoulder-length blonde hair braided on one side. She had oceanic eyes and wore a welcoming smile.

"You, over there!"

The smiling elf skipped toward me from the tree where she stood. She waved her hand to ensure she had my attention. Truly, it wasn't necessary; she already had it.

"Yes," I nervously whispered. She was more stunning up close, and she smelled like an open field of many plants freshly picked, an aromatic paradise swept into a single smile.

"You're a human, aren't you?"

She looked over at my ears. I was frightened now. I read that some fay don't care for humans, but the rumors were rather conflicting and dated. I supposed I'd find out soon enough.

"I am," I stuttered. "I hope it's alright that I'm visiting your kingdom. May I say it's incredible?"

"Oh, it's no problem at all." She tilted her head and smiled. I took an immense sigh of relief.

"What brings you all the way here, though?" she asked me with puzzled eyes. "The next home to humans must be at least fifty miles away from here."

I nodded. "Well, I heard the thread you elves fashion is the best there is."

"That's right." She flashed me with a suspicious look. I noticed many other fay doing the same as the noise faded. "You aren't planning on taking our most prized material and sharing it with the outside world, are you?" Her look turned almost venomous.

I held my breath for longer than I could stand before releasing it all and shaking my head.

"I would never," I told her. "I simply wish to see it for myself. And perhaps ask a few questions if that's alright."

A switch seemed to have flipped. She returned to the smile she wore before, perhaps an even bigger one.

"Fantastic," she said as she took my hand. "Come with me."

"Wait, where?" Before I knew it, I was dragged in her direction.

"You're hungry, aren't you?" she asked. "You have to be, after making the trip all the way here."

I was unsure what to make of her statement. I then felt a rumbling in my stomach and realized she wasn't wrong. I'd carelessly eaten more than half my rations just on the way here.

"I suppose I could eat."

"Of course you can." She tightened her grip. "You arrived just in time for the feast."

"A feast? Really?"

She pulled me through the meandering streets where I could more closely see just how intricate the city's structure was. Each type of wood appeared to have its own purpose, be it for the construction of a home, a mount, a staircase, or a bridge. The attention to detail was superb. The branch woven arch we approached was no different.

"Here we are."

We walked under the archway into an immense hall filled with various fay, some of which weren't even mentioned in my book. There were also long oval tables spanning over a hundred seats adorned with white clothes and a bounty of red wine and local produce.

"I just hope you're not a meat-eater," she said with a smile. "Salads work."

I was so bewildered by it all—not just the food but the architecture and the entertainment. There were statues on every corner. Some closer to the center of what I fathomed to be their ancestors immortalized. Many held circular vases that poured water toward the straights carved into the ground that fed the tree roots forever.

Elves walked with instruments in their hands each way I turned. They played a mesmerizing gentle tune in perfect synergy on flutes, harps, mandolins, and others for the entire hall to hear.

She pulled me toward a table a few feet away from the back, occupied by mostly females. About half of them were fairy breeds. I assumed they were her friends.

"Good evening, everyone," she said. "I'd like to introduce you to my friend here. He traveled all the way here just to learn about our thread."

"Really?" A purple-haired pixie looked at me with intrigue. "Are you sure you didn't come here just for the women?"

"Why would you travel all this way just for thread? You're not a thief, are you?" one with black hair asked.

"No, not at all."

"Good." A tall male elf with green hair leaned his arm against mine, pressing much of his body weight down. "If you were, I'd have to kick the shit out of you."

I gulped and looked the other way. "That won't be necessary."

"Come on, don't scare the guy," a blue-haired fairy said.

"He doesn't look like he wishes us harm." A sprite suddenly hovered over my head. She had red hair and a warm smile. "I think he's telling the truth."

"Yes, I am." I nodded. "I come here as your humble guest. To learn about your sacred thread if that's alright."

I continued to stare down nervously, wondering why I was being left in silence. They then broke into a round of giggles.

"Fair enough." The male elf pulled me upright and patted me on the back. "You seem like a decent guy."

"Yes, take a seat," the female elf told me.

With a bit of unease, I took a seat beside her and had their eyes locked on me the moment I did.

"Now, what would you like to know?"

She poured me a tall glass of wine while the other female elf fixed me a salad from the litany of vegetables around.

"Well." I took a nervous breath. "I read a story about the perfect thread used to forge the string of an elf's bow. With it, their arrows can strike any target no matter the distance."

"Oh, yes," the fairy replied. "You're speaking of the mother thread."

"The mother thread, you say?" I raised an eyebrow. That detail, I knew nothing about. The name perplexed me.

"When an arrow is released from a bow forged out of this thread, its echo is strong enough to reach into the hearts of men and leave the stars shaking," she continued with a glowing set of eyes.

"That's quite powerful," I said, "and a bit romantic."

"Oh, it looks like the human is trying to court you," the pixie said with a grin.

"I think it's the other way around," said the nixie.

"I didn't mean to—"

"It's alright," the female elf said before I could finish. "Just hearing about this thread has that effect on most people."

"Really?" I took a sigh of relief. "And have you seen this thread used before?"

They all paused for a moment, looking at one another before turning their attention back to me with half-smiles.

"Well, none of us has ever seen it," the male said.

"Only the mother fay has access to it," the female elf added.

"And who is this mother fay?"

"She's the progenitor of all our races. It's said she planted this forest's first tree," said the fairy.

The detail astounded me. I envisioned a little girl finding an acorn several hundred years ago and planting it. As the years would pass, the seed would grow into that first tree. I filled in much of the blanks from there, but I imagined she met a man when she grew older. Together, they fostered the many fay races into the prosperous woodland civilization that hangs over me now.

"She sounds like a very impressive woman."

"She definitely is," the sprite said. "We have both our home and our existence to thank for her."

The other fay nodded with smiles of agreement.

"I'm sure she'd be thrilled to know her land is still thriving, and all her people are still celebrating her achievements," I said with a warm smile before taking a sip of wine.

"Well, she isn't dead," the female elf spoke.

I nearly choked on my wine, gasping for breath. "I'm so sorry. I didn't mean to—"

"It's alright." She laughed and patted my back to clear my throat. "It's a common mistake made among humans."

"The few that venture this far, anyway," said the fairy.

"You see, fay like us live a lot longer than you," the pixie told me. "Several thousand years, actually."

"Several thousand?" My jaw dropped. I thought only dragons could live that long.

"Yeah, most of us are over five hundred years old," the female elf said. "Myself included."

"I'm the eldest at over eight hundred," said the nixie.

"And I'm the baby at just over three hundred," the male elf added.

I was so shocked. They couldn't have looked any older than I was, yet their ancient eyes told the truth. This was incredible.

"I suppose I'm the baby here," I said with a nervous laugh.

"You sure are," the sprite said.

"And how old is this fay mother?" I gulped, worrying asking her age may sound crude. "If you don't mind my asking."

"Not at all," the female elf said. "I believe she's around ten thousand years old. A bit of a frail thing these days, but she's still alive and kicking."

My eyes widened. I knew not of even a civilization that lived that long. To think she'd been around to see it all. I was shaking.

"Are you okay?"

"Yes. This is just a great deal to take in. Because of my people's susceptibility to so many diseases, we're lucky to see the age of fifty."

"That's it?" The nixie looked at me in shock, and the pixie elbowed her with a scowl. I assumed she thought it was a rude thing to say.

"What I meant is your people sound so quant," she continued with a nervous laugh.

"I don't know if that's much better," the fairy said.

"Don't worry about it. The problem's mine. You see, I'm a doctor."

"Really? Like a witch doctor?" the sprite asked.

My eyes lit up. "You mean you've heard of my profession?"

"Of course we have," said the female elf. "The fay mother was the first, after all."

"I guess she's still inspiring new generations. Even among the humans," said the pixie.

I lost myself in their incredible revelation. I was truly in awe to be in the first witch doctor's land. "Do you think I could meet her?" I asked.

Their excitement fell silent. Many of them looked away, and I quickly grew nervous. Did I say something wrong?

The female elf leaned forward with a whisper and worry on her face. "The thing is, she isn't very welcoming to humans."

"I see." I wasn't surprised to hear that. Humankind has always fallen short of being hospitable toward others.

"They used to wage war against us centuries ago. Mostly for our resources."

I imagined such wars. Many schools taught children that humans were the heroes always. I envisioned this elder figure leading the fay charge against their greedy adversary.

"I can see why you're so protective," I replied. "Sorry to ask, then."

"Well, it doesn't mean there isn't a chance," the female elf said.

"Really?" My eyes widened.

"She has this very particular way of judging others from the outside. I don't know how it works, but if you have what she's looking for, you can meet her."

"You mean she can read me with just a glance?" I was intrigued. This was beyond my expectations of what I would learn on my trip.

"That's correct," she said.

"And what do you think my chances are?"

"Difficult to say. Perhaps she'll just let you see her if she thinks you're handsome," the pixie said.

"You certainly have the right charm we would look for," the male elf said with a wink. The other fay nodded in agreement.

I blushed and nodded. "And where can I find her?"

"Take the descending stairs outside this hall," the female elf began, "and just keep following the fireflies. You'll find her chamber toward the bottom."

"In that case, I think I'll pay her a visit. Thank you." I ate the last of my salad and rose from my seat.

"Best of luck," they said.

I nodded with a smile as I walked. I then came across an important detail before sharply turning around.

"I forgot to ask. What would happen if I failed to meet her conditions?"

"Oh, if you fail, she'll kill you," the female elf said. My face went even whiter than hers. "But you'll be fine...I think."

I froze with my jaw open for a moment or so. I could only wonder if such perils were worth the chance of quenching my curiosity.

For as long as I could fathom, I'd seen such torment, such loss in the eyes of humanity suffering under the weight of its own ignorance. Their inability to conjure remedies to sickness derived from their unwillingness to engage with species that might help them. As one of those humans, I believed it was my duty to care when others wouldn't. Even though I was vilified, they'd thank me in the end. Even when my life was on the line, I was certain the fay mother would help me see my ambitions through.

I took a deep breath and used the smile they still wore to guide me. I turned back around and proceeded to exit the hall where the staircase awaited me.

Why do these instruments sound like they're playing a dirge for my funeral? I thought.

I found the back door and opened it. Just a few yards to

the right, I saw the staircase she described—wooden steps cascading into the soil with twisting rails and a luminescent glow beneath. I bit back my anxiety and walked toward its brooding presence. Before I took the first step, I looked over my shoulder to see if they were behind me for whatever reason, perhaps to talk me out of approaching the fay mother. They weren't.

I nodded and ventured down the steps, moving deeper into the barely lit passageway below the ground.

As the light from above began to succumb to the surrounding shadows, fireflies larger than my head appeared through the darkness, flapping their wings and guiding the path for me.

I had no clue bugs could grow so large. This city was full of mysteries and the greatest could still be waiting for me at the end of this staircase.

I moved further down for what must have been an hour. In the distance, I could see a pale blue light and the flat surface of a chamber.

That must be her chamber. Now, I suppose I'll find out if I have the credentials she's looking for. And face my doom if I don't.

I took my first step off the staircase. My legs trembled from being off the constant descent and back on solid stone. I crept my way toward the stony entrance, hoping not to disturb her.

Admittedly, I should have been far more afraid of dying. The arrogance of humanity, I could chalk it up to be. But I knew well I was just too curious for my own good. And maybe the fay were right; I could be her type.

I stood to the side of her chamber and peered into the dome-like room filled with books. It reminded me of mine but was far more grandiose. The ceilings were lit with blue luminescent mushrooms that grew from beneath the soil cracks.

In the very center was an enormous bed in which a woman with wrinkled skin and tattered gray hair rested. Her blue eyes could barely open. I knew in an instant it was her, and the sadness of her state had me imagining what sorts of triumphs she must have garnered during her prime.

"Excuse me." I knocked on the side of the entrance. "I don't mean to bother you."

Her eyes turned toward me with a smile. "A human. I haven't seen one in over four thousand years."

I took a deep breath. I wasn't sure how to approach someone bearing so much wisdom and power. Did she already deem me a waste of her time?

"How can I help you, my dear?"

I took a heavy breath to calm my speeding heart. "I heard you're able to manifest this very powerful form of thread."

The fay mother tilted her head and grinned mischievously. "The treasured thread that helped forge the strongest bows our people have ever seen."

"If you don't mind," I muttered. "I'd like to see it."

Her tone grew more sinister. "How many of you humans have we killed thanks to those bows? How many have we sent to the stars with the arrows we launched?"

I shivered at her words. She was silent for a while, and I couldn't tell if she wanted me to give an actual answer. I refused to fathom what would happen if I guessed wrong.

"I'd be happy to offer you your wishes."

My terrified expression softened with relief. I began to smile, believing now that I'd passed her test.

Before I could move, a thread appeared through the air. It was white like the moon and shined even brighter. It connected from her heart to mine. I understood my test was only beginning at that moment.

"But I would need you to offer me mine."

My blood ran cold. I could feel the thread digging deeper, wrapping around my heart. "And what is it you want?"

She smiled at me. "I'm growing old, you see. I don't have much time. With a certain human's blood, I could rectify that."

"You mean—"

"A ritual of sorts," she told me. "I believe your essence will be compatible with mine. I can tell by your eyes you're almost as ancient as I am. You've lived many lifetimes before making it to my chamber."

I had no idea what she was talking about. What other lifetimes did she speak of? Suddenly, images flashed through my mind. I saw morbid creatures swallowing me—a pale one with a vicious howl and one with a jewel. I witnessed a massive storm of orange flames and recalled something being sewn together.

I swore I saw my hands fade into a pale mist, only for a second before waking from my vision. I gasped. I felt a sharp pain in my head as I pressed my hand against it while I still could. I let out a scream and stumbled back when I felt a tugging from inside. The thread was still attached. It made incisions in my heart. They were negligible enough to keep it beating, but I was certain I'd lost a few years from that impulse.

The fay mother looked at me with a wicked smile. "I'll make this more interesting by giving you two options. Give your spare years to me or be given my sacred thread and all the power it holds."

My aching heart raced and hurt even worse as it did so. I was certain she had just offered me her most prized relic.

I looked at her with a puzzled glare. The smile she still wore must have been the one she'd flashed the many humans before me. Normally, the decision would have been easy. I'd take the thread, but I didn't want to do that. I couldn't take away the pride and symbol of a society she'd built and fought to protect.

I didn't want to give my life to her, either. There were still so many diseases left to cure. In the end, I was given the choice to live on and support the humans or die knowing the fay's ruler could continue her reign.

"Alright," I began with a somber look. "I give my blood to you."

"What a selfless heart you have."

With a widened smile across her face and a tugging from her bony fingers, the thread reeled in her direction. It was over in a white flash. Her string coiled around my heart so tightly, she hacked it to pieces. My existence was stopped. Though I supported her will, my end did not differ from the humans that opposed her. I would join all she'd slain over the centuries high over the trees she grew, deep in the stars.

THE WATERING PLANT

The air was sticky as I marched through the thick and vast rain forest, miles from my homeland. I was surrounded by birdsongs and chattering primates on every corner.

The serene night sky twinkled with stars that brought my heart a sense of peace as I traversed this unexplored region.

I still couldn't believe I was on such an expedition. Searching this exotic terrain for the myriad of medicinal herbs it possessed was my version of paradise. There was little telling what I could find. What discoveries I could make.

As I chopped down the branches with a machete to clear a path, I recalled against my delight how I got this opportunity in the first place. The conversation with the king of Elandor happened a week ago. I sat across from the bloated royal in his office, cringing at his unkempt goatee and receding hairline. He had his usual scowl common to our meetings.

"I'm not going to ask you again," he said.

"Then don't."

I leaned back in my chair and thumped my boots on his desk. I hummed one of my favorite tunes while glancing at my fingernails—clean, as always. I thought to bother him a bit more.

He pounded his fist against the desk. I looked up with a grin as his face began to redden.

"Damn it, witch doctor. This is serious. People are dropping like flies, and they need your help."

"You didn't seem so bothered ten years ago when these illnesses made our way into our city," I told him. "Is it because you're worried this will now hurt the Elandor's image?" I looked at him with a smirk as I took my boots off his desk and leaned forward. "That's not it. You're worried it'll hurt that big vault of gold you've stowed under this floor. With fewer people, that's less money."

The king's eyes flared at me. "You disrespectful little prick. My fortune has nothing to do with this situation."

"So, you admit you have an obscene fortune?"

I could tell by the quivering of his lip he was getting especially upset. I was curious to see if he would begin breaking things—a shame if he'd have to spend his own money and not my taxes to fix them.

"This is all just a joke to you, isn't it?" He sneered. He stood from his seat and moved toward the window. I assumed he was looking down at the number of corpses sprawled across the street.

"While we're on the topic of payment, I really think we need to restructure this deal you're proposing."

"I beg your pardon?" He darted his vicious eyes toward me.

"Why is it you pay people more to shovel shit than for me to rid an entire city of disease?"

"Because you're less than shit!" He darted back to his seat, slamming himself down.

"That poor chair," I said as I listened to the seams of the ruby leather tearing. "I fear one of these days your overgrown ass will do to it what your carelessness has done to all the people you pretend to sympathize over."

"Quiet that mouth this instant or I'll have you arrested!"

It was such a childish threat. I felt like I'd taken his toy ship or kicked his sandcastle. I could only sigh.

"All I'm saying is you've been heavily regulating my work ever since you took office. A lot of lives could have been saved if you let me do as I please. A lot more money could have been shoved down those pockets of yours."

He raised an eyebrow. It seemed he was taking me a bit more seriously. That or he was just enthralled by the notion of a larger sack of gold.

"You have to do something," he demanded. "As your king, I'm ordering you to cure these people."

"Look," I told him sincerely. "I'd love to heal these people even if they don't want my help because I know they'll appreciate it in the end. The problem really falls on your shoulders at the end of the day."

"You're the fucking doctor here; not me."

"I know that. However, thanks to your supposed leadership, I've been extremely limited on the sorts of excursions I can pursue due to the low pay. Venturing into lands where I believe supernatural entities live, finding them, gaining their trust, and learning the secrets in hopes of forging cures with materials and methods we don't have access to is expensive. Not to mention time-consuming."

"How about this then?" He leaned forward with a grin. "I'll cover your expenses in full."

My eyes widened. I was almost certain I'd heard wrong. Such an offer would be more charitable than any I'd ever received. I wanted to mock him, but I had developed a strange sense of respect for his sudden resolve.

"There's one condition, however," he said.

My enthusiasm faded. I expected the condition to be very degrading.

"If you can't mend this city of all its illnesses by winter, you'll be exiled from this city. Never to return." He leaned forward with a heinous grin. "Do I make myself clear, mister witch doctor?"

I paused for a moment. Did he just have a stroke? I scoffed with derision and shook my head.

"That's such an absurd condition. Do you even know what you're asking? These illnesses have been around for centuries long before they reached our city. Furthermore, because of my lack of exposure and what I already told you about the time constraints, it would—"

"Yes or no," the king cut me off. "You accept my damn offer, or I'll throw you in prison for your heresy. A man like you would never last."

The amusement on my face washed away. I could tell he was serious. I needed to consider what the greatest cost I'd have to pay would be if I were to fail.

I stood from my chair and put out my hand with a grin. "You have yourself a deal, you bloated bastard."

The king rose with a grin and shook my hand. "Excellent."

I recalled that smile he had at the end of our exchange as I walked through the rainforest at night. It was clear this was an elaborate way to get rid of me. Truthfully, I was better off exiled than imprisoned for the other option would require I remain in his walls until I rotted or committed suicide, as he would have hoped for.

I clenched my fists. Though I enjoyed getting under his boil- and hair-covered skin, it still hurt; not just because the townspeople want nothing to do with you, but when their highest authority wants you out of your own home.

Essentially, I was starting over. I knew there'd be no way I could do it in time. I'd have to build a new home here with the few books I managed to stuff in my bag and hope against any odds I could find the cures I was searching for in the surrounding herbs.

I moved further down the trail I was clearing. The sounds of the apes grew louder, and I saw the faint silhouettes of snakes slithering across the branches and tigers stalking the ground.

There were predators each way I turned, beasts searching for their next meal and hoping to take advantage of those without night vision.

I had to set up camp. I couldn't do that anywhere here. I need to find a place where I'd be alone, even from the animals, but was there such a place?

As I proceeded, staying rather cautious of my precarious surroundings, I saw a plant sprouting from near a bush I immediately recognized.

"*Camelia Sinensis*."

My eyes lit up at the sight of white petals crowned with golden anthers and oval green leaves spread wide. It was a rarely exported plant in Elandor. Though most would use it with tea, it had potent healing qualities. With the right creature to help me surpass its potential, maybe an elf or a fairy, this could be the start to finding my first cure.

I was filled with elation. I kneeled and reached for a handful, seeking to take all of it with me. Suddenly, a pair of predatory eyes appeared in the shadows.

I gulped and carefully backed off as the yellow spheres drew closer, stalking me. As the creature stepped into the light, I recognized the golden mane and glistening canines flashing at me. A thundering growl burst into chilling roars as the lion stepped out of the shadows.

Sightings of this beast were so infrequent in this terrain. Naturally, my luck would have it I'd run into one.

"Easy," I said in a softened tone before stepping back. "We're friends here. I don't want to hurt you. I just want a bit of these plants here."

The lion looked to where I pointed. I was sweating bullets, hoping he could somehow understand me. I had a terrified and nervous grin. The lion made it clear with a ferocious growl that it couldn't be persuaded, and then it pounced.

I nearly lost control of my bowels as I released a scream. Just before he could strike, there came the shout of a woman's voice in the distance.

"Enough, sweetie."

Sweetie? Was she speaking of the lion? Surely not.

She then came out from the shadows. I could have sworn she was one of the trees. She was nine feet tall and had an earthy complexion, limbs that resembled roots, and hair that glimmered a deep green like the leaves.

The lion aborted his attack and marched toward her. She looked down at me with a callous set of eyes.

"What is it you're after?" she asked.

I was so astounded. This was no fay I'd read about. This was a fabled dryad said to protect the earth. She was more humanoid than I expected. They were depicted more like trees in my texts, but she resembled a very slender woman.

I was in awe of her beauty. She was like a goddess carved out from the forest, staring down at me. I then remembered her question. The scowl on her face told me she'd rather not wait.

I nodded while regaining my composure. "I'm a witch doctor. I'm here to see if I could harvest some plants here in your forest."

"And why would I let you do that? I'm the guardian of this rainforest. I take men like you who rape my land of its resources and crush their skull against the stone for my animals to feed!"

This would not be easy. Fortunately, I believed I could strike a compromise with the dryad.

"I respect your forest, along with your desire to protect it. It's your home, after all."

She raised a leaf that resembled an eyebrow.

"You see, I was exiled from mine. I'm looking for a new place to settle and continue my research."

"Out of the question."

"Hold on."

I didn't expect her to reject my proposition, especially so quickly. I was sweating again before the woman more terrifying than any lion.

"I won't cause any interference. I only wish to find a cure to humanity's greatest illnesses."

"Is that a fact?" she looked down at me with a nefarious grin.

"My species is in danger. I know you don't have a vested interest. Perhaps I'm your enemy. Just name what it is you desire in exchange, and I'll offer it to the greatest of my ability."

"I can name anything, you say?"

She leaned forward until we were eye level with our faces just a foot apart. I could see her stone and soil-like face up close. It was mesmerizing as the distance between us was frightening.

"I suppose you could name anything," I said with a gulp.

"If what you say is true, then." She stood up straight and turned her head toward her left. "You'll be my apprentice."

"Excuse me?" I was baffled, to say the least. What would working for her entail?

"You'll help me maintain the ecosystem in this land and receive a place to stay and do your work in exchange."

My eyes widened. "But why me? I trespassed on your sacred territory and angered your animals, did I not?"

I stumbled back slightly as the gazes of many veracious wild beasts still lingered around me, salivating as I gulped.

The dryad responded with a playful grin. "Let's just say I have a fascination with humans. Perhaps I'll even conduct an experiment of my own. What do you say, Doctor?"

She leaned closer to my face. I could see every detail of her earthy complexion like the soil forging a mosaic of a stunning woman. I considered and concluded that it was a fantastic offer. A dream manifesting in my waking life. I had no issue accepting it.

"When do I start?"

"Now." She chuckled. "This way."

I didn't know where she'd be taking me. She led me down a path she carved out with just her steps. The trees in her way would succumb to her presence and the animals would walk beside her from afar. Fauna of all different breeds marched under the protection of a single rain forest spirit.

It was so enchanting. We walked on until we came to an extensive structure in an open spread of land. It resembled a greenhouse, but without the glass or roof—only a variety of plants within the walls, along with other dryads.

I marveled at the countless flora as we approached the botanical chamber's door.

It felt more like a garden with a very high gate I couldn't see over now that we were closer. She opened it and let me in. I was faced with the sight of endless rows with endless species of any plant I could think of and possibly more. More importantly, the potential was in the dryads around me. These towering women of the rain forest could be the breakthrough I needed. Forming a bond with them could be the key to finding all the cures I needed to preserve humankind.

"You'll be staying in the spare bedroom under these grounds," she told me.

"No problem at all."

I examined the slew of plants on the shelf nearest me—large fly traps consuming swarms of bugs in an instant.

"Don't get so excited. Your bed is just a patch of dirt. That's what dryads sleep on when we don't hibernate in trees."

I nodded with a fading smile. "Understood."

A few other dryads took notice of me. They sneered with derision, eager to make a hostile advance, when the dryad next to me shook her head left and right as a signal to leave me be. They begrudgingly continued with their work.

"Before we begin this evening's work, I'd like to ask you a bit more about yours, if you don't mind."

"Not at all," I said. I was a bit taken aback by her sudden interest. I thought little it. Given our new arrangement and the aversion most had toward what I do, it'd be best she'd learn about it now. "As I mentioned earlier, I'm a witch doctor. I study supernatural entities like yourself in hopes of strengthening ties, but also in learning of ways to forge more effective remedies for the many illnesses taking a hold of my people."

"You certainly came to the right supernatural kind," she said with a smirk.

I nervously laughed. "Yes, I suppose I was very lucky I was exiled here."

"So you were," she said with a grin.

Around me were the sounds of plants swaying against the wind and the buzzing of flies being eaten by pitchers as the dryad stood over me in silence.

I began to grow nervous and veered my attention away. "Why do you ask?"

"Is that a problem?"

"It isn't," I replied. "I just worry I may come off as someone with an ulterior motive. I assure you I don't wish you harm."

"Yes." She smiled. "You told me that before."

Her tone shifted into an eerie and unsettling register that had my heart speeding a bit. She seemed almost too trusting now. I stepped back.

"Anyway, you won't have to worry about it being a hindrance. You won't even notice I'm working on my practice. I'm the reclusive sort."

"Oh, there's no need for discretion." She stepped toward me, closing the distance I tried to create. "I'd be happy to help you cure humanity of its greatest illness."

She was growing less trusting by the minute. What were my choices? I couldn't run away now that I was in her territory. I could only cross my fingers and hope she didn't have an ulterior motive, either.

"If what you're saying is true," I began with a tremble. "Your help would be invaluable. Truly."

"Well, that makes me thrilled to hear." She leaned forward. "Let's get started now. You can help me feed these aloe vera plants. Tomorrow morning, I'll tell you a few ways we dryads harness some additional power out of them."

My eyes widened. I was lulled by her suggestions.

"Yes. I think that's a good place to begin if it's no trouble."

"It's my pleasure."

I nodded with a bit of lingering reluctance. She forged a stepping stool out of wood with the roots from the ground. With it, I could water the plants on the same level as she was. Together, we began our work.

I used a wooden pail she placed by my side. She looked at me with a smile as she handed it over. I assumed she crafted it the same way she did the stepping stool. Regardless, I was pleased by how helpful she was. Her smile was rather nefarious, like something a succubus trying to lure in her pray would wear. Perhaps I was wrong. Perhaps all she wanted was something lower than her to dump her dirty work on. Perhaps she could be trusted.

I began watering the plants, listening to the sounds of water splashing against the spiked narrow stalks. The feeling was peaceful. I could see myself being regularly entranced by the tranquility.

I looked over at her with a smile. "I greatly appreciate this. You're doing me a wonderful service, but also a service to my people."

"I know I am."

"Though they can be a nuisance to many, myself included, I know they can change once they see the value beings like yours can bring."

"Oh, I don't see that happening."

"Excuse me?"

I was hurled out from my elated trance in fear. I saw something moving from the ground—thorny vines of many plants heading my way. In seconds, I was tethered by the wrists and ankles. I gasped as they lifted me over five feet in the air.

"What is the meaning of this?"

I looked at all the elated grins of the other dryads before locking with the one who brought me here. She stared me down, and the look on her face promised malice.

"I told you I'd help you cure humanity of its greatest illness."

"Then, why—"

"You see, humanity's greatest illness is humanity itself." From the ground were two more stalks with thorns at the tips flashing their reflection at me. "And it's time I rid your people of that disease."

I was mortified by the betrayal. I couldn't move without the thorns around me digging deeper. I couldn't bring myself to plead for a way out. She'd done enough and so had my people. They were the ones who exiled me in the end. If she hoped to also slay them, that would be fine.

The two stalks rushed toward my eyes, blinding me on impact. The thorns penetrated my brain, and it was over. They were at liberty to infest all of me and make me a part of the forest if they desired.

And like that, I was punished not for my practice but for being blind to the true scourge in this world.

SKELETONS AMONG
THE HERD

I wandered past faded headstones, sunken tombs, and dry shrubbery. How did I get here? The air was so cold and thick with fog. The last thing I could remember was falling asleep after reading one of my favorite books on undead literature. Was this the product of some strange dream I was having? Was any of this real?

I kneeled and reached for the charred ground beneath my feet. The dusty gravel crumbled with my slightest touch, and I jolted back. My eyes widened when I realized I could experience its morbid embrace.

I began to breathe rather heavily. Perhaps this wasn't my imagination, and I actually was walking through the land of the dead. I rose to my feet, hearing the crackling against the dried-out soil. I looked all around me. I didn't notice them before, but on closer examination, I could see pale silhouettes moving through the fog.

They were faceless, with ambiguous limbs swaying. They appeared to be wandering aimlessly. My hands shook at the sight of them. Just where had I been taken?

I looked down at my hands. They lost their tangibility,

turning translucent against the moonlight. My heart skipped a beat. This sensation felt so familiar; like my muscle memory reacting to its surroundings. Soon, I found myself becoming one of them—a specter in the night.

Memories of how it happened seeped in: only hours ago, I'd awoken from the ground, screaming and gasping for breath as I tore my way out of my premature burial. Or was it? Was this the afterlife?

I looked over my shoulder and saw the deep chasm from where I'd pulled myself out. My fingernails ran deep in the soil.

"What the hell is this?" I mumbled. "How did this happen? I was just fine the other day. I was reading. How did I die?"

Panic struck me as I stumbled in every direction. My body's state sifted between corporeal and less so as I became more tempered, more terrified of this horrific reality I'd been cast into.

I suddenly felt my heart stop. I wasn't dead again; rather, it felt as if I was starting over. My body began to return to its original state. I took a sigh of relief, yet I had no idea what had just happened.

I examined my surroundings closer. I appeared to be alone with these ivory apparitions. All that accompanied us was the wind and the rustling of branches on decrepit trees. I couldn't see much else. No buildings. No city in sight.

If I was dead, I was certainly far from home. Who buried me then? Why was I taken to this resting ground?

I was beginning to think none of my ailing questions would ever be answered in this ashen wasteland. I took a deep breath and continued to move. Perhaps I could find the answers I sought if I walked through this macabre terrain.

I left where I'd found myself behind and moved into the terrifying unknown, hearing each heavy step I took. I reached the specter hovering around me. I wondered if it knew I was here. Could it see me as I saw it? Could it hear me at all?

"You, there," I nervously began. "Can you tell me where we are?"

The apparition didn't seem to pay any mind. I couldn't tell where its face would have been. It was like watching silk dance in the shadows.

I think I'd been given my answer in its silence. Now was a bigger question that, amidst the shred of composure I was gaining back, harkened to my years of researching such phantom-like entities.

"Just what would happen if I were to reach my hand and" —I spoke as I moved my hand toward the ghost. Just as I'd been told in my readings, my hand went through its exterior with no resistance. It was like breaking through a cloud. Yet, I didn't feel wet; only colder. Much colder.

The ghost didn't react to my embrace. I doubt it could even notice, for I believed it was beyond the world I knew. Still, I feared the frozen touch it gave off.

They barricaded me in every direction. If I was to progress any further, I'd have to walk all the way through these creatures. As if taking a plunge, I held my breath and strode forward. Each step became quicker than the last as I sprinted through the first ghost.

My eyes widened at the chilling sensation. I was being drowned in both the cold and the sorrow of the spirit. I felt its tragedies—experienced the mistakes and agonizing life it once had. It all coursed through me as if I was its vessel. I raced for the other side, taking unbroken strides to escape the sensation until it was over, and the night was my sole companion.

I looked ahead now. There were no ghosts for miles ahead; there was this utter emptiness that didn't bode well with me. I was missing their company now, chilling as it was.

I asked myself if perhaps I was better off never moving. Maybe the ghosts were trying to keep me safe from this abyss in decay.

I weighed my options—to step back and wear their tribulations all over again or move forward and hope solitude was all that awaited?

I nodded and took my next step. Solitude wasn't so bad; in fact, I preferred it. That's the one certainty I could still hold on to.

I moved on, leaving the ghosts to dance on their own. Everything was so quiet now. And so much darker.

I underestimated the light the ghosts provided. I could hardly see my feet moving across the ground. An inky smog blanketed the ground. It was far too dark to read, even if I had a book with me. All I could do was lose myself in my thoughts.

My mind took me to this fascinating read I recalled during my early teens—a story I sampled in the library once about banshees. They were a more potent and sentient breed of ghost I always admired. I wondered if I could spot any here.

My mind was then injected with an image of one—a face I remembered seeing by a nunnery I'd never been to. None of it looked familiar, but it felt as if it had somehow happened. A bloodcurdling howl nearly knocked me to the ground, and everything soon vanished.

I gasped with terror, just barely maintaining my balance. It felt so real. Just what was it I saw? Why did I feel like I was seeing it again? My head began to ache. I couldn't hold the pain back as I grunted and screamed.

Like a hammer crashing down, I was pummeled with more images I couldn't recall. I saw a ballroom of vampires silencing me with a vermilion jewel and a man on an island setting me in his flames.

I gritted my teeth. These visions were absolutely ceaseless and originating from a place I didn't know.

"Stop this. Please!" I screamed. "Whoever you are!"

I felt my mind being manipulated by an outside force for reasons I still couldn't comprehend. Perhaps it was the night playing tricks on me. Perhaps the memories of the ghost's heartaches still lingered inside me?

I began to hear voices. The visions were speaking to me, looking back at me with faces I'd never seen.

"This is a very special sort of marriage, you see."

"I saved you so that your soul could be mine in the end."

The voices toppled over one another like a maddening symphony fighting for the spotlight and my mind, the stage, collapsing. I began to shout, squirming under the moonlight. This had to stop. This had to stop right now, but how?

"You've lived many past lives. I'd like to take all those years of yours and add them to my own."

The voice came from an elderly woman in a tree. What fucking tree? Who was this damn woman? And why was I so convinced or what she spoke of that these tragedies were always mine to wear?

"You don't remember me, do you?" His voice nearly stopped my heart. The cacophonous band of raging thoughts ended, and everything went quiet. I could see his face. His horns. This was a man I knew. My mind told me that, but my eyes couldn't recall him.

Where did I meet this man? Where did I meet any of these people and what were they talking about?

All around me was the milky translucence of faces beyond. None of this made any sense. I saw the face of an older gentleman that looked like me. His smile was so pure. There were small children who seemed to know me. Did I know them from long ago? I could hardly make out their nefarious eyes through the growing mist, through the pale tempest of spirits dancing in an inescapable hex. My mind rattled under the weight. I ached under the growing mass of disembodied whispers.

They're so hauntingly familiar. If I've truly encountered these people, how could I forget their passing? How could anyone?

"Perhaps I can be of service to you." I jumped out of my skin from the sudden voice. I knew it didn't come from my head. I was comforted only by the fact I knew I hadn't heard.

I turned toward my left and faced a man I was certain wasn't there before. Where did he come from just now, and was he the one toying with my mind?

"Who the hell are you?" I exclaimed.

The man turned toward me. I couldn't see his face under his thick green hood; only a blackened mist.

"The truth to this pandemonium in your mind is what you seek."

I was taken by his brooding tone. It resembled almost that of a snake if one could speak. He didn't move an inch from under the barren willow tree where he stood. It was as if he was waiting for me.

"Maybe it is," I cautiously replied. "What do you know about the truth?"

"I know quite a lot."

The man dug under his ragged robe and revealed a deck of cards with a green back and a black pentagram containing an image of lightning bolts coursing through them. I recognized them as tarot cards.

"I don't much care for readings."

"Oh, I insist." He raised his deck forward as if gesturing me to walk over and pick the cards myself.

I'd always been skeptical of readings. Though my love for the occult adored the idea, all the readings I ever received were bad luck. I began to think it was just a clever way of conspiring against me.

The man didn't leave me much choice. He wouldn't move even a finger from his bony gray hand. There was no one else in sight, and I feared my mind could attack me again at any moment. *I suppose a reading wouldn't hurt.*

I walked toward the man. Even as I moved closer, I couldn't see anything but a cloud of darkness under his hood.

"A wise decision."

I nodded toward the deck in his hands. "Normally, the reader chooses the cards."

"No need to worry. I already have."

Three cards slid forward through the deck. I darted back with a slight gasp. Was this just magic he performed? Who was this man?

"Don't be shy," he told me. "Your fortune awaits."

My lips quivered in fear now as I reached for the top card. Was this some sort of trap he was luring me into?

I took a card and looked down at the image. It was of a man lying prone on the ground with many swords lodged in his back.

"I see you've drawn the ten of swords. How troubling," he said.

I didn't need him to tell me that. I may as well have been the one in the picture; I'd seen this card in my readings so many times. In fact, the longer I looked, the more he began to resemble me.

"This card is telling me I've hit rock bottom. Is that right?"

"Very perceptive. Though it could mean many things. Perhaps you've been betrayed by a loved one recently...victimized over the way you choose to be, and you were left powerless in the end."

I shuddered as he spoke. I knew this prophecy well. Each day, I lived with the feeling—a city of people that despised my line of work; a family that abandoned me because I chose to be a witch doctor instead of a precious soldier. I gritted my teeth. Tears ran down my face at the sight of their swords digging deeper into me.

"Are you ready for your next card?"

I took a deep breath and nodded before slipping the one I had back on the bottom of the deck. I grabbed the next one protruding from the deck.

I took one look at the image and my eyes immediately widened. This was a card I wanted to see. But how could he have known that?

"Ah, you've drawn the tower. A favorite of mine."

I looked down at the image of a black tower with a looming background. From the top window, a man was being tossed out. Once again, I felt I was staring at myself in this card, plummeting to my demise.

"This card signifies a sudden change you've experienced. Perhaps one you were blind to for a while."

My heart pounded with a sudden flashing of the images of before. Why was I bound to them? Was this man right? Was I changing into something I couldn't understand? What the hell was happening to me?

"The lightning bolt at the top represents the path to a hidden truth. Follow it and you'll unravel a life-altering revelation."

I stared down at the green lightning bolt and the sight of me falling toward the ground. I felt so much despair each moment I gazed upon the image. Still, I yearned. I yearned for this revelation he spoke of.

I placed the card on the bottom of the deck and reached for the last card sticking out. I stumbled when I looked at the image. For a moment, I swore I was staring into a mirror. I wasn't. It was the face of a man with purple horns.

"Your last card is the devil." The man chuckled and gazed toward me. For a moment, I think I saw a semblance of a face, blackened and hallowed out. I felt my blood running colder than before.

"Please let me draw again," I whimpered. "That can't be my fate."

"I'm afraid the card's chosen you. Besides, drawing the devil isn't so bad."

Was this hooded menace trying to feed me shit? I'd never heard of anyone desiring that card in their reading. I would know. Often as I would draw towers and swords, I never once had a reading without the devil.

"What this card tells me is that there is a very toxic sort of relationship in your life. Something putting on a great strain."

"I know," I said. I was shaking with anger. "I get harassed every day for my work."

"Oh, it's not about your work."

My eyes widened at his claim. How could he know, otherwise? What else could he have been referencing? I had no acquaintances to speak of.

"In this case, I believe what happened is you made a deal with someone long ago. A very malicious deal you're still paying for."

My mind flashed to a very early childhood memory: dusk hung over the city streets of Elandor as a towering man with the same horns in the picture approached me from an alleyway with a smile on his face. I looked back at the card, and it was the same man.

I stared blankly as my jaw dropped. My sanity was being violated, taken over by some heinous force. I couldn't recall much from this encounter, yet it felt so real and dire in the consequence of that evening.

"Look now at the man and woman on the bottom of the card."

I was possessed by my despair and confusion. My eyes

turned toward the image's bottom as he inquired. I saw two naked figures with pink flesh and black and white hair.

"They represent the desire and shamelessness you have—a recklessness in your pursuit for what it is you want."

"But what do I want?"

I couldn't figure it out. Why was I seeing all these images and hearing these voices? They became more familiar each time, like they'd been screaming out for me for many lifetimes. And just who was that man I saw when I was a child?

"What do you think?" he asked me. "Was this fortune to your liking?"

Fortune? He took the card from my hand and shuffled it back in the deck before moving toward me. I could plainly see a grin devoid of remorse underneath his mantle. My look of shock slowly molded into disgust.

"Get away from me."

"I cannot," he told me. He placed his deck back under his rags and reached out his bony fingers. "There was a cost to revealing your fortune; a payment required to collect for my master. The ruler of this decay."

"What cost do you speak of?"

My heart pounded out of my chest. The man slowly dropped his hood to reveal a face seemingly crafted from charcoal. There were no teeth or eyes; just a flattened surface with sparse indents to represent a face. The black mist poured around him.

"The cost is your soul."

His body began to manifest beyond what I already deduced to be inhuman. He rose to an incredible ten feet in stature, a towering silhouette with swaying arms. He was like a demented scarecrow attempting to pounce. I shielded my face as I screamed. My return to this soil was imminent when there came the sounds of barking.

I turned to my right, where two colossal wolves rushed

toward us. Their fur and flesh were absent; they were composed only of bone. How they were animated was beyond my understanding.

I jumped out of the way just before I became their next meal. The two wolves pounced on the hooded giant, smothering him to the ground. They tore at his rags and ripped into his flesh. He hardly put up a fight beside the infrequent jolt. He bled a misty green as his black aura faded into the shadows.

"This is not the end of you, my friend," the man said to me as the wolves gashed his face. "Nor will it ever. You've been warned."

Soon enough, the wolves silenced him when they finished feeding on him. I feared I'd be next as I trembled and backed off. To my surprise, however, they rushed in a different direction, toward the sounds of snickering.

I looked over and saw two young girls. They had silver hair of differing lengths, brown skin, black dresses, and bones across their attire. They raised their arms out to the wolves, hugging them with delight.

"Very good boy," the one with the short hair spoke.

"Hopefully, that nasty underling learned a lesson for trying to double-cross our papa," the long-haired one spoke.

Papa? I thought. *They couldn't have been speaking about me, were they?*

I turned toward their smiling faces. They looked back with surprise, like they'd seen me before.

"Hey, it's you," the short-haired one spoke. "You're that witch doctor."

I shuddered at their knowing me. How was it possible anyone would know me in a place like this?

"How did you know I'm a witch doctor?" I pressed. I was losing patience now with all of it—the visions, the voices, and whatever amusement someone was getting out of this. My face started turning red. "Tell me."

The girls looked at one another with flustered glares before turning back to me.

"You mean you really can't remember us? Talk about rude," the long-haired one spoke.

"I guess that's one of the side effects," the other one said.

Side effects? Were these brats in on this, too?

"If only I could forget that dumb story he told us," the long-haired one said. They laughed in agreement.

I clenched my fists. I needed an explanation for all this. I didn't even know where to begin.

The short-haired one looked back at me. "Sorry about that underling before. He should have known better."

"Our papa should be here to make things right," the other girl said.

"And who is your papa?" I asked.

"Oh, yes," the short-haired girl replied with a grin. "We lied to you before."

"We do have a papa and he's the ruler of this decay."

They were so convinced I'd met them; I was starting to believe it. When from the sky came a flash of green lightning.

I shielded my face from the crushing intensity as the ground before me was stricken. I could hear a rattling of bones and a cackling in the storm. I creaked my eyes open to welcome whatever awaited.

There stood a man, seven feet tall, with a body made of bones clad in robes. He had a long beard and a green crown. He stared at me through eyes made entirely out of the bolts that summoned him, grinning back at me.

"I know what you are." I trembled as I recalled the many readings depicting such a regal undead. "You're a lich."

"The lich king," he corrected. He stepped forward with

such finesse. Such purpose. The ground coursed with electricity and shadow. "I heard you were keeping my girls company not long ago. I thank you, but I've come here to take what's mine."

"What are you talking about?" I shouted.

The lich king looked at me with a grin before digging under his robe. I half expected another deck of cards. Instead, he pulled out a box crafted from bones and flesh. In the center was a green, veiny eye.

"This is my phylactery," he began. "As a witch doctor, I'm sure you're acquainted with these."

I certainly was. How could someone in my practice not have been? They were the most prized vessel of his kind, the archetype of their power and their lifeblood.

"You keep those hidden well, don't you?" I said. "Deep beneath the soil. Even in alternate planes."

"You're rather astute. This one, however, I kept buried in the heart of a fierce dragon from another land."

I gulped as he spoke. I could tell he was serious.

"I decided to let my old friend have his favorite calvary back so that you and I could make a deal."

Everything was happening so fast. Someone was seeking to rob me of something each way I turned in this decrepit wasteland.

"I'll get straight to business," he began. "Your immortality excites me. Quite a bit, in fact. And I want to know how you acquired it."

Did he just refer to me as immortal? If anything, *he* could live forever. I was fairly certain I'd died and was hurled into this grotesque afterlife to be doomed, recalling unfamiliar memories I couldn't escape.

"You have the wrong man. I'm only a human."

"I don't." He spoke fast and with great conviction. "It appears you don't know if that's the answer you're willing to give me. I can only assume the friend of mine I mentioned earlier must be responsible."

"What friend are you speaking of?" I muttered.

"It matters not. I've summoned you here because I desire your soul. With my phylactery, I will have it."

"You want my soul?" I exclaimed.

My heart nearly stopped. There was no chance of escape. What options could I have against a lich king? His box's eye stared at me, glowing brightly.

"That's correct. With it, my influence over the spirit world will grow. Consider your sacrifice a great honor, for your spirit won't be destined to wander like the others. It'll be enslaved under my command."

The ground began to shake. I could see streaks of pale white seeping from the fissures. Against the odds I was facing, my heart was still defiant. I couldn't die a restless spirit no matter where I went; I had to take whatever chance and fight for my right to closure.

"I refuse," I told him. "You can't have what isn't yours. Not until I get what I want."

I flashed a smirk in his direction, hoping it would intimidate him or at least change his mind. The scoff he returned told me rather differently.

"I'm afraid that isn't an option. I've made many sacrifices to get to this level of power. I gave up my life on the mortal plane. I even lost my beloved consort."

His daughters looked down with sullen expressions, appearing to remember the passing of their other parent.

"Your time is up. The lich king always gets what he wants."

From the ground came numerous bony hands. Clawing their way out were skeletons in the hundreds, turning toward me. Their bones rattled bones, and they cackled with delight under the guile of their king.

"Now, my dark servants. Make him one of your own!"

I was cornered. The horde of skeletons marched closer, shrinking the gap as the two girls snickered with delight.

I took a deep breath and clenched my fists, refusing to go down without a fight. I prepared for a battle against his legion. In moments and not any later, I saw just how outmatched I was.

They grabbed me by either hand and pulled me toward the ground. I flailed back and forth, but there were far too many. I was deep in their morbid embrace. They grabbed at my limbs as I felt the sinew tearing. The mass was swallowing me and screaming for help was pointless.

"Plead all you wish," the lich king said. "Only the devil can save you now!"

He summoned a skeletal horse beside him and mounted it as if claiming a triumphant victory.

The devil?

I recalled the tarot card and the many flashing images of horns, and finally the tall man I met in childhood. I still didn't understand—as my body dragged and ripped to pieces, I believed I never could, not in this life or the next. Perhaps my destiny was to be a slave to my ignorance.

I was down to my last limb as the bony faces looked up at me from the ground. My heart slowed. It appeared there really were no answers for me—none that the world could give me. No. This was not my destiny. I couldn't allow suffering or the hands from the grave to win. If the world wouldn't give me closure to my unrelenting demands, I would take it myself wherever I would go. And the devil, I would find him.

THE LAND OF FIRE AND
BLASPHEMY

How many days had it been? I honestly couldn't remember. I'd been walking through this hell and hadn't seen another soul. *What's happening to me?* I yearned for the company of another for the first time in ages.

I was surrounded by purple molten rock. Trees crackled under the smoldering heat of the ember-clad air. The flame-spewing mountains hung high into the writhing clouds as my lungs filled with smoke, and I coughed profusely. My fingers bled as I attempted to catch myself with my hand.

"Where are you?" I grunted.

My chest tightened as oxygen grew thin. I still didn't know where I was or how I ended up there. Somehow, I knew it wasn't the first time; the memories held on this time. I realized I'd been sent to many different places before by methods still beyond my grasp.

"I know you're here...watching me...laughing at me now, but you won't for long. I swear it, devil!"

I began to piece it all together despite struggling against my sanity to complete this insufferable puzzle, unable to distinguish what was real from what wasn't.

I started with the two flashing images pressing hardest against my mind: the image of two women dressed in red and white, respectively. I recalled their seductive grins. They were alluring by their own method. Considering their conclusions, a shriek and a glowing stone respectively as well and not a second more, my time must have ended with them in tragedy.

Whoever these women are, it's clear I met them. But when could this have happened? I don't remember.

Their blazing red eyes drew closer in my mind—like molten suns from which my temptation could not look away.

I clenched my fists and took a deep breath. *I'll need to retrace my steps, somehow. Starting with the one I met first.*

I tried to better recall the whole of my experiences. I remembered being taken to a meadow of banshees. We drank tea under the moonlight and danced the night away.

I recalled a different night with vampires. Their paranormal delights were clearer now. I remembered being taken to a ball where I was proposed to and deceived. How? I wasn't sure. I could only see a vermilion stone before the image of a vampire's fangs and a flash of light. The images stopped, and I was left with the hell before me.

"That was less than helpful," I muttered. "Still"—my eyes widened with a sense of hope—"they appeared in that order; never overlapping."

I rushed to the nearest stick I could find. I bit through the heat of its touch and began to draw into the stone. I started from my left, moving to my right. I carved in the banshee's face and drew the vampire's face beside it.

"Alright," I said with a smile. "Some progress, at last. There were other memories, however. Following this theory, I'll just need to draw them as they appear and hope there's an answer waiting for me in the end as to where I am."

Another vision flashed where I was taken into a cellar full

of demons. I came across a chamber with three bodies stitched together. I could somewhat recall their faces—good sign. Whatever black cloud was blinding, my memory appeared to be subsiding.

A fiend stood before me by the door and grinned maliciously. He appeared to be out for my misery.

"You won't have to worry about losing your friends. Now, you'll always be together."

My eyes widened as the vision ended. Were those three people friends of mine at some point? What happened to them to end up in such an egregious state? My stomach churned at the sight of their corpses sewn together. Resentment swelled toward the fiend, whoever he was.

I dug my stick deep into the ground to carve his face beside the vampire's and took a deep breath to calm my nerves. How could I, really? It was obvious I'd encountered some wicked people and there were still memories to go.

I remembered sailing into a storm and being attacked by a horde of mermaids before a man with orange hair coming in to save me. A slight smile formed on my face—perhaps not all these people were terrible? The vision ended with a roaring organ flame that nearly knocked me off my feet.

My eyes widened. I shook from the intense battle against my mind I just lost. I was wrong. Though he saved me from being violated, he had his own ambitions of doom. Those I still couldn't see. Those of a dullahan.

As I carved his face beside the fiend's, I began to wonder why these visions ended so abruptly. Were they trying to tell me something?

My mind fell into a truly repugnant vision. I felt as if I was being punched in the gut and groin. I let out a vicious scream before kneeling over and vomiting across the carving of the fiend. It was so vivid...so potent, as if the very fabric of my recollection were laced with a drug killing me from the inside.

I recalled a circus where I was a jester and many demons performed to a crowd of humans. I saw a ringleader, a lumbering figure whose grin tore at me without hesitation.

Blood splattered against my recollections. Images turned red as I remembered an idol, half-eaten bodies, and the sight of him in the courtyard, grinning down at me in a field of mist with those alluring eyes.

It ended—one of the worst sensations I'd ever felt. I was hunched and shaking as I carved his face beside the dullahan's.

I then remembered something else. Another vision. This one had dead bodies, skinned, and hallowed out. The last image had me numb to the brutality. I then saw two little girls with troubled, yet mischievous, faces; they must have favored the latter. The vision ended with a violent storm of green lightning.

"What the fuck is going on?" I clenched my fingers across my head. "Why can't I see how these end?"

I carved their faces beside the devil. I could only cross my fingers; I'd see the conclusion soon enough.

Another image appeared—this one was of a scavenger hunt. I was rather perplexed. Why was I looking at myself collecting odd objects in the woods?

I was then brought to a ritual I performed to summon a castle. I found myself in that castle with a carnivorous man resembling an owl. Just who or what was he? Why was I facing another cannibal?

The image ended with a chamber filled with giant infantile owls. He had me hanging over the ledge and that was it. It didn't take a doctor to realize I was murdered.

I think I'm understanding this now. My eyes widened with joy.

"That's fucking it. At the end of each of these visions, I died."

I grinned as I carved the face of the owl beside the faces of the two liches. Soon, I remembered how they all really ended: being aged to death by a banshee, sucked dry by a vampire, gashed and stitched to a fiend, burned by a dullahan, eaten by a devil, stricken with lightning by liches, and eaten again by owls.

The puzzle to my madness. The damn pieces. It's been solved!

I soon lost all comfort this revelation brought me. I was dying each time at the hands of a monster. Why?

The air grew hotter, almost under the flames. Smoke covered much of my vision as I continued to unravel my thoughts.

I recalled another memory of townspeople chasing me out of a bazaar. Shortly after, I encountered a black market selling illegal merchandise. I then ran into someone by the shore—a towering red man.

"A fomorian," I muttered.

I remembered touring an underwater mining shaft and later drowning while he escaped with the others escaped.

I carved his face beside the owl's, thinking more about just what sort of deathly hand I was constantly being dealt.

I recalled what felt like a paradise, entering a fay village. They were all so beautiful and vibrant. I remembered sharing a meal with them and not wanting the experience to end, yet it did.

I saw myself walking down a musty path filled with fire-flies, where I found an elderly woman resting in her bed. She tied a string between our hearts—I couldn't recall why. She pulled the string her way, and I was killed.

Watching myself die over and fucking over again didn't bring me any pain or sadness, merely a growing emptiness. I carved her face beside the fomorian's, hoping the next vision would be simply dying in my sleep.

I saw myself walking through a rain forest where I encountered predators that told me I wouldn't have what I sought. I then met a tall woman made from the trees—a dryad. She took me to her home, a place filled with botanicals. It felt like a dream again to have the cures I was looking for in my grasp.

Her voracious plants, however, grabbed me by every limb, digging their thorns into me before striking me in the eye.

I shook with terror as the memory passed. I quickly regretted realizing my fate each time as I carved the dryad's face beside the fay mother's.

I was exhausted. How many times could I watch myself die? My mind ached with all sudden images. I took a deep breath and stepped back to examine what I'd gathered so far. There were ten distinct visions, it seemed. Ten times I died. Why was I always dying?

"You've reached the bottom, my friend. With the ten of swords."

My heart skipped a beat at a new memory. It disappeared before I could see how it ended. Could I have been witnessing a vision that didn't end with my death?

Something pulled deeper me into the vision. I saw the man who spoke those words revealing tarot cards. I saw skeletal wolves eat him and a lich appear with the same little girls as before. I then came to a realization. A question grasping my mind like the hand from a grave.

"If I've truly died, who was responsible for bringing me back?"

I witnessed as he called forth his legion of undead beasts from the ground. I could only assume this was how I would die.

But the image was interrupted by the grinning face of the devil I drew. I gasped at his purple glow. I saw the horde of vixens that tried to seduce me. I saw the sea of ochre dead smothering me. Lastly, I saw his die roll on the number six before I was sliced in half, left to an underwater grave.

"That was him. The devil. So, he's killed me more than once."

The interrupted vision returned. The skeletons tore at my flesh. I shuddered as I watched my arms and legs leave me and my entrails pour out. I was dead not long after and the lich king grinned.

He approached me on his horse with his phylactery, which glowed and grunted as if hungry for something I had. Before he could reach me, another man appeared in a cloud—the devil.

I saw a second tarot card—the tower. Was fate about to be redirected?

The two figures began to battle over my remains. I watched purple flames clash with green lightning until the fight came to a swift end with the devil's victory. He knocked the lich king on his back and siphoned something out of his phylactery, but what? And why was he grinning? Just what did this encounter mean? I knew I was seeing it for the very first time, but the other images were memories. I was shaking. Each step closer to understanding my fate was like tripping several steps back.

I was shown a third tarot card—the devil, coming to life in my mind as his hands reached out for me.

I shouted and stumbled back, running as far as I could through the black void of my subconscious.

"Enough of this. I know you did it," I shouted without realizing or with much understanding of why I said it.

He grinned back at me, flashing his teeth. "You can't hide from me. Your absolution is a contract written in blood."

I was knocked out of my nightmare and found myself on

my back, gasping in cold sweat as I looked up at the purple sky.

That was just a dream. Or was it?

"If the world won't give me closure, I'll just have to take it myself."

My eyes widened. The voice that appeared in my mind was my own. It spoke with such clarity. I didn't have to dig for it.

And the devil. I will find him.

"That was also me." I rose to my feet, disoriented. I stumbled around, trying to grasp what it all meant.

"I need to start from the beginning. It's worked for me so far," I said with a grin twisting on my face. "I was killed by the liches twice and the devil twice. The question is where they fit in this timeline I've created."

I looked down at the line of ten faces with a flustered look. I wiped off the dust and vomit for clarity and began to dig my stick into the ground.

I started by wedging the devil's face in between the fomorian and the mother fay for a second.

"It felt about this recent, right? I'm pretty sure I was cut in half just after I drowned and just before I had my fucking heart sliced to pieces."

I could feel my sanity slipping. I didn't care. I didn't need it!

"And I was killed by the lich king all the way down here."

I scribbled his bony face beside the dryad's. I cackled with amusement amid my accurate yet sloppy design.

"Yes, he must have just tried to kill me. I received my fortune that same lifetime just moments before he tried to take my soul. But wait?"

I remembered how this vision ended—with the lich killing me, yes. But with him failing to secure what he desired.

And the devil, I will find him.

"That's it." I broke out into a laugh. "He's behind this all. The devil in the motherfucking details, ladies and gentlemen."

I'd never been so amused or enthralled by anything, and nothing could ever top this. I made sure I could be heard from the mountains. I even began to hurl my fists, my feet, and my head against the trees and stones. I cackled to the purple skies with the maddening conclusions. My blood spilled, but none of this mattered because the devil did it. I would always die because of him. And something also told me he'd always revive me. Why? I couldn't care less!

This was truly a blessing in the disguise of so many curses. At last, I knew my fate was in his hands.

Another image in my mind appeared that left me frozen in silence, robbed of the bliss I'd worked so hard to scavenge. I saw myself standing in that alleyway with him, extending my hand toward him.

"So, it's a deal?"

"That's right."

What was it I saw? Was that our first meeting? I was beginning to understand where this timeline started to fray. I made a deal, didn't I?

I could hear singing in the distance, muffled by the sounds of a crowd heading in my direction.

"What a delight when a mortal succumbs. The contract is signed, and a new friend is mine."

It came from the mountains. I stared with flaring terror in my eyes as gargantuan spiders with purple flesh stampeded down the slopes. Upon them were large, purple devils with their red eyes locked on me.

"All hail the diabolic fire. A rebirth, your soul, in exchange for your desires."

Two figures seemed to lead the charge—a woman singing the odd verses and a man singing the even.

"But now is the time to collect. Your days, your wishes and all your dreams come to an end. You made a wrong turn at the fork. This is your final story. Your life is taken, and our hell is yours."

The devil's army stopped just a few yards from where I stood. I was so perplexed; dizzy as the manic episode I had begun to take its toll.

"That was a pleasant song," I muttered. "But who are you?"

The male and female looked at one another with smiles. They stepped off their spiders and approached me.

"Nice, indeed, but it doesn't seem you were listening," said the female.

"Your time has come, and our master is yearning for you," the male added.

They towered over me by two feet. Their grins beat down at me like a dark sun as the skies swirled around them.

"Your master, you say?" I took a deep breath. "You speak of the devil I formed a pact with. Is that right?"

Their eyes widened, astonished by my assumption.

"Your memory serves you against the odds."

"Surely, you recall the conditions of your deal, then," the male said.

"I don't. Only that I made one and that I've been paying the price ever since."

"That can't be possible. No one forgets the deal they make with our master," the female devil exclaimed.

"Well, I forgot a great deal more than that if you can believe it."

"I can't say I do," the male said with a disgruntled set of eyes.

"Come this way, and I'll show you what I mean."

I walked toward the sloppy timeline I drew. I heard slow footsteps following just after. I walked toward the drawing of the banshee's face and pointed down the line with my stick for them to see.

"My first time I recall dying began here. The last ended on the other side."

"We know how timelines work," the female said.

"And you don't need to keep pointing with a stick. We aren't children."

I didn't know what they wanted from me, then; I gave them an explanation of what I knew. I was clear as I could.

"That's everything I have thus far," I told them as I caught my breath. I looked up at them with a tired smile. "If I recall anything else, you'll be the first to know."

"I must say it's rather impressive you can recall the exact order," the female said.

"Thank you," I spoke in a lofty tone.

I think a chord in me must have snapped. If I were to become any more nervous before an entire army of giant cannibals and their web-slinging cavalry, I'd break into a nervous laugh and soil myself afterwards.

I cleared my voice before starting over. "Thank you. I wrote them down in the order I could remember. Not much more. Any others that appeared, I wrote by what felt more recent."

They both looked down at the drawing of the devil's face wedged between the fomorian's and the fay mother's, unimpressed by my explanation.

"Do you think you're living in a dream?" the female asked.

"Those battered fists and that idiotic smirk tell me you don't believe the severity of your situation."

"I believe," I replied earnestly. "I made a deal that leads to me being reincarnated and suffering many deaths. I know it's real because when I saw those visions, I could feel them."

"It doesn't bother you, then? Dying so many times?" the female asked.

I took a deep breath and put on one of the sincerest smiles I'd had in the longest time; just having it made me feel lighter.

"There isn't a lot I can do in the end. I can only hope whatever I received in exchange was worth it."

I proudly nodded with my answer. I really was understanding the situation. Now it was time to get out.

"The contract I entered with your master as a child. Where is he?"

"You're stupid and eager, I see," the female looked at me with a grin.

"Neither. In fact, I have a level of clarity I haven't felt in ages. In any lifetime."

"I suppose that's rather fortunate for you," the male told me. "What good will that do you now?"

"I'd like to speak to him regarding this contract. In particular, revoking it."

They both stared at me in stunned silence. The devils waiting idly behind them broke into a laughter they both soon joined. I was baffled, to say the least, and I felt insulted. Surely, one of them could be bothered to silence themselves.

"You want to break a contract with a deal? Our leader?" she said.

"I believe that is what I said." I sighed.

"They don't work that way, I'm afraid." The male laughed.

I was growing impatient. I didn't want to deal with his cronies any longer; I wanted the belligerent fool to show himself, wherever he was.

"Look, I made it when I was a child. I don't even remember the conditions. Obviously, he still has a very vested interest. Otherwise, he wouldn't have taken my soul away from the lich king in the last lifetime."

They looked at one another with more serious expressions as the laughter subsided.

"It's only fair we end whatever arrangement we have. I don't know what I was hoping for all those years ago, but all I want at this moment is to go back to the day things were. My homeland and its people await me."

I was firm on my answer and tired of being met with the same grisly fate. I'd gone desensitized and such a feeling didn't sit well. No matter how extravagant the offering I received from the devil, it was time we ended it.

I then heard roaring flames above me, and the clouds twisted in a tempest of pure fire. The devils and their spiders skittered off in the presence of whatever lurked in the sky. The chaos cleared to reveal a barbed tail and beating wings.

Its body descended—the smooth underbelly of a dragon a hundred feet from jaw to tail. It flew from over the mountains with its flaring eyes set on me. I was so in awe of the majestic terror of so many legends. Its scales and flesh glistened against the backdrop of flames. As the distance shrunk, I saw a man mounted on its head: the devil to which I was bound.

A large expanse of molten stone cleared for his arrival as he landed, seated upon his ferocious beast. I was so mystified; not by him but by the colossal beast I'd only dreamed of seeing.

I couldn't dream now, however. I couldn't afford a tangent, for I had a seal to break. He stepped off his dragon and walked toward me.

The other devils kneeled in his presence. Even their spiders showed their respect by lowering their heads.

Before me was the man from long ago, the figment of many of my nightmares returning, standing with the same grin.

"Rumor has it you want to break the contract we have."

"Word spreads quickly on a dragon, it seems," I began. "Yes. I think our agreement has run its unnatural course."

"But just as you said, this is an agreement we have."

He leaned forward and placed his long talons over my shoulders. The grin he wore, no matter how many times I saw it, left me shaking.

"And an agreement with a devil is a river that runs forever, never to dry out even in your wildest fucking nightmares."

The mist around him blackened. I shuddered as the surrounding air grew so hot I thought I would melt.

"Be that as it may, I believe an exception should be made here as I don't even recall the conditions of our deal."

"And is that my problem?" he asked me with a grin.

"I think it should be. Just what could I possibly have that you'd want to keep so vehemently you wouldn't even consider my words?"

He raised an eyebrow with intrigue.

"More importantly, what could you have given me? Life certainly hasn't gone my way. Not for as long as I can recall," I continued.

"Is that right?" the devil asked. "Please tell me each detail."

I snarled at his unapologetic sarcasm. It was apparent he was amused by my suffering and my helplessness in his devilish hold.

"For one, I was picked on for all my schooling years. Even university. My parents threw me out of their house when I was ten."

"Oh, what a travesty. At least you lightened the bullshit a bit. Why stick around when everyone fucking hates you?" he asked.

I sneered, ready to hit him. "My entire life, each one, I was ridiculed for being a witch doctor. I was underpaid, threatened with imprisonment, and even exiled in one life.

So, tell me: what aspect of that could I have possibly wished from you?"

The other devils went silent with looks of concern on their faces. Perhaps they were afraid of the frank tone I used to speak with their leader or how he'd reply. Whatever the case, this needed to stop.

"You know," he began. "You're quite flippant, given your predicament."

"Are you saying I should be more upset than I already am?" My face began to redden. "That shouldn't be a fucking problem."

"Take a closer look, my friend. You're far from home...in a rather turbulent environment, I might add."

I glanced at what I already knew—a purple hellscape with corrosive magma spewing and skies shaking.

"And?"

"And you stand before an army of devils, their leader, some rather gigantic spiders, and a dragon."

My eyes began to widen as they took stock. Still, what was his point?

"Aren't you at least a little afraid? How can you challenge me with no hesitation or regard to consequences?"

I smirked. "The same way I've faced every creature before you. It's for my love of the supernatural."

"Oh?" He grinned.

"I've loved studying all sorts of entities like yourself since a child. In fact, it was my dream to always meet one."

"Was it now?"

I looked up at him in bewilderment. He was telling me something. Then, it hit me: I was a child, all alone in a dark alleyway and crying with a book in my hand. The children I thought were my friends hurled rocks at me, even as I cried.

"Why don't you read an actual book?"

"Freak!"

Their insults rang in my mind as my tears dripped onto the pages of my favorite book on supernatural entities.

"I know they're real. Even if you don't believe me," I whimpered. I glanced down at the image of a devil. His lore, I admired the most. "One of these days, I'll meet one and you'll all be sorry."

"A day like today?"

I jumped from my skin. "Who's there?"

To my left were heavy footsteps in the shadows. My heart pounded as I slid forward. A man just like the one in the picture appeared.

"No way." I looked back at the page to make sure I wasn't seeing things. "You're a real devil."

"In the flesh," he replied.

I rose to my feet with excitement. My eyes twinkled at his eminence. He was even more impressive up close.

"I have so my questions. Like, is it true you make deals and give people anything they want?"

"Perhaps it is," he said with a mischievous grin. "And what is it you want?"

My eyes widened. "I want to meet all sorts of beings just like you...and make friends with them."

"Is that all? I suppose in exchange, all I ask is you shake my hand."

A thick purple mist emanated around his hand as he extended it for me to shake. I gulped to calm my concern that there was something my mortal eyes could never find hiding in that mist. Still, I didn't want to miss this once-in-a-lifetime opportunity. And with the shake of his hand, I made the biggest mistake of every lifetime.

The dream ended, and the nightmare continued to unfold. He stared back at me with malicious, darkening eyes as he chuckled. My blood ran cold. I was truly unable to break away this time. Even death couldn't save me.

"You got exactly what you fucking wanted in the end," he said. "You met a myriad of different species. You befriended each one. And in the end, they killed you. Each...fucking...time—sending you down a never-ending fucking spiral."

"Murderous comparisons. What an egregious trick," I muttered.

That was all I could think of. An image from a time long ago appeared in my mind. It was the face of a man whose coarse shoulder-length hair and bearded face I could recognize. He wore a welcoming smile even as I traversed the path of a fool who'd made a deal with the devil.

"Dad?" I whimpered as if I was a child.

The memory of his passing from a disease ripped through my heart. My life and memories faded into darkness that day. That was until now. Blood flooded with the image of my slaughter; the gazes of mythical allies dozens of times—hundreds perhaps over many years ever since the deal was made.

"No. This can't be possible." My breathing nearly stopped with the realization. I lost all color in my flesh. "I've been lost in this cycle all along, being killed for my intrigue over and fucking over again. Why?"

The horrific curling grin that formed across the devil's face only stung deeper into my wounds.

"You only appear to remember the most recent handful of encounters. Perhaps that means my shadow's become especially potent."

"Your shadow."

I finally remembered the inky figures in alleyways. Whether I was on my way to be betrothed or solve the veracious genocide running rampant, that lumbering image persisted. That devil stood there each time, watching me with a sadistic gaze in his eyes.

"Yes, my shadow. Your sweet calamity."

He dug his nails into me. I could feel my heart beating out of my chest as my blood trickled down his fingers.

"You've been dying quietly every day since we struck that deal. All out of your own intrigue. Since you'd appear once more with no recollection or injury, your remaining loved ones were none the wiser. They never knew of your pain, but I knew. And now, so do you."

"Make this stop. Please. I'm begging you."

"You're a rather funny one. Perhaps it was because of your youth," he began. "You chose endless lives of ridicule. You were always a martyr for the things you were so passionate for; you forged a deal with the devil."

"I didn't know what I was signing up for. I was a fucking child!"

"I gave you exactly what you asked for, and it's over now."

"What do you mean it's over?" I shouted.

My lips quivered with fear. Surely, the tears I shed couldn't have changed his mind. His smile told me he had no interest in dissolving our contract.

"As my underlings most likely tried to tell you before, the conditions of your arrangement have been met and it's time for me to collect."

He opened up his trench coat. Under his left arm was a number glowing in purple flames: six hundred and sixty-five.

"You may not realize it because your mortal mind has long been overloaded, but this is the number of times you've died since our deal was forged and with your next death, my number appears, and your soul will be mine."

This was worse than death, shelving the hundreds of other deaths I still couldn't hope to recall. I'd be forever a slave to the unrelenting and unapologetic beast before me. What could I say? What could I do to fucking save myself?

"Let me live this life, then. Just a little longer. Let me be happy once," I pleaded.

"That wasn't in the contract. Your time is up." He released his fangs and grabbed either side of my face.

"Let me ask you one last thing before you're finally mine. Was it worth it?"

He clamped his fangs and smothered me in his diabolic embrace. It was over. The contract was complete. I was never to return, and all I knew, all I loved or hated, was infernally his. So ended my story. So ended the final tale...of Alexander Grimlock.

ABOUT THE AUTHOR

J.J. Egosi is an emerging author of dark fantasy and the writer of the Demonheart series.

Grimlock Tales is an anthology of many macabre machinations in my upcoming anthology exploring the dangers of one's curiosity.

COME LEAVE A REVIEW

I f you enjoyed this anthology, please leave a review. I love connecting with my readers and want to know what you feel about my stories. The more reviews we have, the more readers will find my work.

Writing for you is my dream! Thank you for making it possible.

JOIN MY MAILING LIST

If you'd like to stay updated with all my upcoming releases, sign up for my newsletter below. I'll see you there!

HTTPS://DASHBOARD.MAILERLITE.COM/FORMS/333290/ 80484803848176726/SHARE

LOOKING FOR MORE?

If you enjoyed my approach to crafting stories, and wouldn't mind a tale more fantasy driven, I urge to to explore my flagship series, Demonheart. It follows a man just as lost in his mind while he attempts to grapple what's sound him. The main difference, however, is the story centers around demons and angels. With that comes a larger than life storyline spanning a world just as immense. Follow the link below and you can embark upon the first 3 installments in these primeval escapades.

DEMONHEART- BOOKS 1 TO 3